TWO DAYS EARLIER
London

"I am leaving soon I promise," Penny whispered into her mobile, and in a drunken haze clutched the bannister and walked up the stairs, her long black dress swished behind her. She looked down at the party below, everyone out of their heads on drink or drugs.

"Jason, your time will come," Penny angrily whispered to herself, she swayed down the landing and made her way to the bathroom.

A man approached her.

"Penny isn't it?" he had an accent, dark hair, and olive skin. He was on the large side.

"Yes," Penny slurred, trying to focus on the man's face.

"It's me, Carlos, you, and Jason, were on my yacht, you do not remember me?" He gently placed her hair behind her ear. Penny pulled away from him.

He smiled at her, and Carlos walked off and said loudly "I don't know why Jason has such awful taste in women..." chuckling to himself.

Penny glared at him and forcefully opened the bathroom door, the white marble floor glistened under the spotlights. The gold taps gleamed. She faced the mirror

1

and looked at herself.

"Roots need a touch-up," she sighed and lightly pulled at her blonde hair, she hiccupped and leaned forward and gave a smile. Penny looked behind her and totted over to the loo, her Jimmy Choo's clattering on the marble floor. She lifted the lid, glanced out of the window, and saw two men, frog-marching a man down a path. She took a step closer to the window and peered down. The two men pushed the man towards the garages at the far end of the garden. It was a warm summer evening, the white flowers glowed under the security lights. Jason, her boyfriend, only had white flowers, no colour.

Penny was about to sit down when she saw Jason storming across the lawn. He joined the two men; she could hear raised voices. Then Jason pulled out a gun.

CHAPTER 1
Oban

Penny wiped the misted window of the car. Six months ago, Penny met Jason, he swept her off her feet, with his expensive cars, and his mansion in Southwest London. Penny asked what he did for a living, and his reply "This and that". It never crossed her mind, it could be illegal, though she was blinded by his wealth. Penny was not naïve, though any man who had a huge bank balance was worth the risk.

A few days ago, Jason hosted a glamourous party, and Penny witnessed Jason shooting a man. Jason was not aware she saw this.

Penny managed to get to the police and because of Jason's criminal history, the police wanted a conviction and decided to place Penny under the Witness protection programme until the trial.

Penny reluctantly agreed. She was not allowed to tell her parents or sister. She only had ten minutes to pack a suitcase and then she disappeared. The police were taking Penny to a Scottish island, though they did not tell her which island it was.

Penny sat in silence in the car waiting for the ferry, Oban was bleak on a cold summer's day. The policeman turned to her.

"You will be fine, once you get to the island, you will be quite safe," his accent was from the Midlands, he was quite nasal, which grated on Penny.

Penny looked at him and then turned away.

"Have you read your file?" he was tapping the steering wheel with his fingers in agitation.

"Yes, my name is Penny Hargreaves and I moved to the Island, as I am a journalist and I am researching a book on the Scottish Islands," Penny sighed and looked down at her hands, not quite believing the situation she was in.

"I know this must be hard for you, though just think once a trial date is set and he is banged up for good, you will be able to go back to your old life," he gave a weak smile.

"I want my old life now, I am going to get a coffee, do you want one?" Penny was rummaging in her bag for her purse.

"Oh no you don't," the policeman locked the doors.

"Hey, I am not the prisoner here," Penny protested and threw her bag to the floor.

"Yes, but for your own safety, I ask that you stay in the car until we get on to the ferry," he rubbed his face and gave a frustrated sigh.

"Fine," Penny looked out to the sea, the waves were rough. She took out her phone and turned it on.

"How the hell do you have your phone? They should have taken that from you." He grabbed it and switched it off and put it in his pocket.

"Excuse me, but I need that," Penny lunged forward and

tried to take the phone.

"Get your hands out of my pocket or I will..." he shouted

"What will you arrest me?" Penny gave a sarcastic smile.

"You might as well wear a sign around your neck, saying come and get me, bad guys," he gave a slight snort.

"What is your name again?" Penny snapped.

"Fred," he said quickly

"Fred please can I have my phone?" Penny said in a pleading voice.

"No," Fred turned his head.

"Fred please I won't make any calls on it, I promise," Penny clasped her hands together.

"Seriously... do you realise what will happen if you turn it back on, it's like a beacon and your location will be compromised Penny."

"Do I have to stay in the car for the crossing?" Penny flicked a fly off the window. Fred turned on the engine, as a man in a Hi-Vis jacket was ushering them to move forward.

"Nope," He was peering over the steering wheel, trying to navigate the car up the ramp.

The ship was groaning and huge bangs from the cars driving up the ramp, it was deafening. Fred turned off the engine and undid his seat belt. Shouts could be heard from the crew, directing cars.

"Just wait here," Fred slowly got out of the car.

Penny watched as he walked around the car, he was scanning the deck. Fred was in his late thirties a little on the big side and unfortunately was not good looking. Penny wished Fred had been a hunk for a protection officer. It certainly would have been all worth it. Instead, she has PC Blobby. He came back to the car and opened his door and leaned in.

"All clear, you can now get out," he gestured with his thumb.

"Yes sir," Penny gave him a salute.

He rolled his eyes at Penny and slammed his car door. Penny walked up the steps to the deck above and wandered to the back of the ferry. She leaned over the railings looking down at the sea below. The rain had stopped and even though it was mid-June it was freezing.

"Fred," Penny said walking back to him.

"Yes," he was looking down at his phone.

"So, you can have your phone?" Penny stood with her arms folded, her blonde hair blowing in the wind.

"Yes, I am special," he had a glint in his eyes and walked away from Penny.

"Yes, quite special," she whispered under her breath. She quickly followed him.

"I have no clothes and I didn't pack any thick jumpers, do you think Amazon, will be able to deliver out to the Island?"

Fred stopped and walked back to Penny.

"Penny once you get to the Island, you will have no access to the internet. You cannot draw attention to yourself. I am sure there will be clothes shop on the island," he whispered.

"Sorry, what do you mean by no internet access?" Penny stood with her hands on her hips and flicked her long blonde hair over her shoulders.

"Oh, this is going to be the longest four hours," he said throwing his hands in the air and walking off.

"Fred," Penny shouted.

She marched over to him, and grabbed his arm. He stopped and took a deep breath and slowly turned around and gave her a fierce look.

"You will be fine, obviously Gucci has not opened a shop on the Island, but I understand tweed is very fashionable up here," he said giving a strained smile.

"This is hell, I want to go home, I don't care anymore," Penny was panicking and held her chest.

"Penny you are not going back until we say so... You have only been in the protection scheme for...let me see," Fred looked at watch.

"Eight hours," he was desperately trying not to shout.

"I hate you," Penny yelled and stormed off.

"Feeling is mutual," Fred whispered under his breath.

The ferry left the port, Penny watched the mainland slowly disappear. The sun was now coming through the clouds and the sea was a turquoise colour. She breathed in the crisp sea air, the spray of the sea now and again splashing against the side of the ferry. Penny was in turmoil, she thought it might be best if she rationalised the whole situation. She furiously played over scenarios in her mind, how this could end. She concluded for her sanity, that maybe she should look at this as one long holiday. She would not have to go to work, her rent was paid for, and her savings had been transferred to her new account. Then Penny panicked about her family and would she ever see them again.

Penny spent most of the time avoiding Fred for the next four hours. Eventually land was in sight and Penny turned to look at Fred. This was it, her new beginning.

"Penny time to go" Fred pointed downwards.

Penny reluctantly walked to the steps leading down to where the car was parked, a feeling of sickness took over her. She opened the car door, sat down, and put her seat belt on. Fred was still dithering and taking his time. He was checking his rear-view mirror and then leant over and rustled in the side compartment of the door and pulled out some sunglasses and placed them on his head.

"Welcome to your new home," he said cheerily and drove the car off the ferry and the sign said, "Welcome to Stonbray".

Penny's heart sank. She had been put on an island she had never heard of. Penny turned around still looking at the sign and wishing she was back on the ferry. Driving along the coastal road they drove through some villages and then Fred pulled the car over onto the side of the road.

"Why are we stopping?" Penny was looking around; they were in the middle of nowhere. All you could see were miles of beach and a long road. The wind ferociously blew across the car, at times it rocked.

"We are here," he looked out the window and there was a tiny cottage. An old man stood at a gate, his white hair blowing in the wind.

"What do you mean we are here?" Penny looked around.

"This is your new home; well Croft I should say," Fred raised his eyebrows.

"You must be joking," Penny scoffed.

The croft could have been pretty. The walls were whitewashed, though all the paint was flaking off. A few tiles missing from the roof, and the PVC windows looked like they could fall out at any minute. The drystone wall surrounding the property had collapsed in places and behind the cottage, there was a hill with sheep grazing. A dead rose bush was blowing in the wind by the front door.

"You will love it; you have an amazing view," he said and opened his car door, Penny grabbed his arm.

"I can't live here," Penny was almost crying.

"You can," he pulled his arm away.

Penny watched him get out and he walked up to the man. They started to chat. The old man was not saying much, Fred seemed to do all the talking.

Penny slowly got out of the car and walked up to them. Tiptoeing through the mud, her high heels were not ideal.

"Ah Penny this is Alec, he is the only one on the island who knows about your situation. Alec is your man if you have any problems. He will contact us; you cannot contact us directly," Fred wiped his brow with his sleeve, the sun was now beating down.

"Nice to meet you, Alec," Penny put out her hand to shake his, she was trying to be cheery.

"Aye," Alec said gruffly and raised his hand.

"Have you lived here long?" Penny gave a sweet smile.

"Aye," he said again Penny glanced over at Fred who gave a nervous smile.

"Right, I will get your suitcase out of the car and then I have to get going as I am catching the next ferry back," Fred hurried to the car.

"Fred are you not staying?" Penny gave a puzzled look.

"No, why would I be?" He frowned, his forehead creased, and he was beginning to sweat.

"Well don't you protect me or something?" Penny demanded.

"You mean I sit on a chair outside your cottage all night and day?" he walked back to her.

The sand from the dunes swept over the road.

"Yes, something like that," Penny stood with her hand on her hip.

"You are on your own now …lassie," he said grinning.

He pulled out the suitcase and dropped it on the ground.

"Right any problems let Alec know, you will get a hired car, but that won't come until tomorrow. Remember to sign your name as Penny Hargreaves. Alec will take you into the town to get some things, try not to bring attention to yourself… Oh, and here you go," and he threw a packet at Penny, she looked down and it was hair dye.

"What am I to do with this?" she said looking at the colour which was a dark brunette.

"You need to change your appearance, so before you go anywhere dye your hair, something I am sure you do regularly," he said laughing and opened the car door and got in. He wound down the window.

"Penny someone will come and visit you in a couple of weeks," he gave a quick smile and then drove off.

She watched the car driving down the road. Fear took over and she collapsed to the ground crying.

She was wailing, Alec walked up behind her, watching her crying clutching the packet of hair dye. Penny looked upwards; wiped the tears from her eyes and stood up and wearily walked over to her suitcase and dragged it along the path.

At the front door, there was an overturned plant pot, the green paint was flaking off the door. Alec slowly walked up to the door and turned the pot over and picked up a key. He then slowly stood up and rubbed his back. His slowness was starting to irritate Penny.

"Let me," Penny hovered her hand over his. He glared at Penny and mumbled something and put the key in the door and turned it and the door creaked as he opened it. He ushered Penny in, and they walked into the sitting room. The sitting room consisted of a sofa, and a chair with a table. It had a fireplace and an extremely basic kitchen at the back of the sitting room, and it was freezing.

"Alec, where is the bedroom?" Penny was frantically looking around the room.

Alec pointed at the sofa.

"Seriously I cannot sleep on that," Penny threw the hair dye onto the sofa in frustration.

He slowly bent over and pulled a flap and it turned into a sofa bed. Penny sighed and sat down on the chair.

"Right Alec let's change my hair colour," Penny clapped her hands.

He held his chest in fright and then gave a disapproving look.

"Alec, where can I find some towels?" Penny stood looking down at him.

He looked up at her and pointed over to a cupboard and then looked down. Penny walked over to the cupboard and opened the doors and there was one towel, a sheet and a pillowcase and nothing else. Penny picked up the towel and smelt it, it was horrible. It had that mildew smell.

She walked over to the sink and opened the packet and quickly ran the dye through her hair. She came to sit next to Alec. He nervously looked away and tapped his knee with his finger. All you could hear was the clock on the mantelpiece ticking steadily, and the soft rolling roar of the waves outside, the silence between them was excruciating.

"So, Alex," Penny said cheerily.

"Alec," he said with a frown.

"Sorry, Alec… anyway how big is the island? I had never heard of Stonbray?" Penny sat with her hands on her lap, the dye was starting to sting her head and she frantically scratched her head with the towel.

"Five miles, by five miles," he said looking towards the small kitchen.

"Small then," Penny sighed.

They sat in silence for another ten minutes.

Penny stood up and walked over to the sink in the kitchen and washed the dye out of her hair. She watched the purple water going down the plughole, and clumps of hair, which was slightly alarming. Penny towel- dried her hair and went to get her brush from her bag.

She stood in front of the mirror above the mantlepiece and brushed her hair, it had turned such a boring brown, with some shocking orange highlights. Penny did not care. Who was there to impress on this backward island? She threw the brush down and turned to Alec.

"How do I look?" Penny turned to look at Alec, he gave a weak smile.

"That bad hey," Penny flopped down on the sofa.

He did not answer.

"Where can we eat? I am starving?" Penny stood up and looked down at Alec.

"Douglas Point," he said with an air of irritability, at times his accent was incomprehensible.

Penny picked up her bag and walked to the front door and turned to wait for Alec. He slowly stood up and shuffled towards the door and once outside, he put the key back under the pot. Penny walked to the road and looked around for his car.

"Alec where is your car?" Penny said in a desperate tone, ruffling her hair to try and get it to dry, as it was making her shoulders damp.

"Don't have one," he mumbled.

"Right ...so how do we get into town?" Penny was exasperated with Alec now.

"We walk," Alec slowly walked down the path, a few seagulls were circling the cottage.

Penny stumbled on the uneven path and came level with Alec.

"Excuse me, Alec, how long does it take to get into town?"

He stopped and looked down at her high heels "In those about an hour" he said slowly and was almost smiling.

"Listen I can't walk and carry things, is there not a taxi?" Penny tilted her head at him.

"There is only one taxi," he softly said.

"Only one taxi on the island?" Penny turned and looked out to the sea.

"Aye," he carried on walking.

"Well call him," Penny demanded.

"I can't…" Alec turned to look at Penny, he sucked his teeth.

"Do you not have a phone?" Penny came closer to him.

"Aye," he said again

"Well, where is it?" she demanded.

"At home," he mumbled.

A car came towards them and slowed down and stopped. Penny could not quite see the driver. Alec walked up to the driver's door, and they started to chat. Penny was curious and walked up to Alec and the man in the car gave her a quick smile. He had jet-black hair and blue eyes, he was very striking, he had high cheekbones and was about Penny's age. He raised his hand and drove off.

"Who was that?" Penny watched the car drive off.

"Ethan," Alec mumbled and walked off.

Penny looked out to the sea and sat down on the side of the road. She could not deal with this anymore. As soon as she got to civilisation, she was going to make her way to the ferry port and go home. She did not care about the consequences.

"Missy, I need to get going, I have to get back to my house, ...this year please," Alec said curtly.

Penny reluctantly stood up and brushed her jeans down and followed Alec. They walked down the road, Alec then turned down a path.

"Where are you going now?" Penny said shouting at him and throwing her hands in the air.

"My house," he shouted.

They eventually got to the bottom of the track; a small cottage was nestled in between some woods. There was no road as such, just sand and gravel. The cottage looked more like a shack. Penny watched him go into a large shed at the side of the cottage. Then an engine started, he opened one door and then slowly walked over to the other door. It was excruciating the slowness this man possessed Penny thought to herself. He walked back into the shed huffing and puffing and then out he drove a bright blue battered Mini. Penny gave a surprised look and walked to the driver's side. Alec had the window down, Penny leaned in.

"I see, was that some sort of joke about not having a car?" Penny squinted her eyes at him.

"Aye," Alec did not look at Penny, though she could see he was smiling.

15

Penny quickly opened the door and got in, the thought of civilisation, was exciting.

"Alec, can you recommend a good hairdresser?" Penny was emptying her high heels which were full of sand.

"There is no hairdresser on the island," Alec said slowly.

Penny sat back in her seat not quite believing what he was saying.

"Right...well can you drop me off at the nearest Costa coffee?" Penny stared at Alec.

"No Costa on the island, or anything else. Ellen has the only shop on the island...." He sighed.

"Hold on lassie," Alec sped off, a cloud of dust following them down the road.

CHAPTER 2

For someone who moved incredibly slowly, Alec made up for it by driving fast. Penny leaned over at one point and saw he was driving at 70 mph. Alec had his window down and his white hair was blowing all over his face. He was frail, probably in his late seventies. His eyes were blue, but sunken, his complexion ruddy.

"Sorry Alec, can you slow down a little," Penny said looking up trying to find the handrail above her.

Alec ignored her and raced along the coastal road. They eventually came into the town. He screeched around a corner, almost running over a cyclist. He parked the car and was trying to get out. When he eventually stood up, Penny thought to herself, if she were to be in any sort of trouble; how on earth would he be able to help her or protect her? Then the thought of Jason finding her, sent shudders through her body.

"You ok, lassie?" said Alec now showing some gentleness.

"Would you be?" Penny said curtly.

"I guess not, let me take you to Ellen's shop. She has everything you will need and while you are here, I suggest you buy some sensible shoes. Today may be dry though when it is wet, it is wet and those contraptions on your feet will not help you," he was now back to his gruff old self.

"Fine Alec, you are the boss," Penny said through gritted teeth.

He ushered Penny in the direction of a shop across the road. Penny stepped out into the road and a car came screeching to a halt, she clutched her chest in fright. Dazed Penny stood there, and the driver honked his horn. Penny looked at the driver and realised it was Ethan, the man they had just met. He leaned out of the window.

"Look where you are going," he snapped and honked his horn again. Penny stepped back onto the pavement, and he sped off.

"What is his problem?" Penny turned to Alec, he had walked off and was now standing outside the shop.

Penny quickly ran across the road, looking both ways this time and caught up with Alec. The shop had a cream exterior and hanging baskets on either side of the door, filled with wildflowers. Above the door was the sign *"General Store"*. The bell above the door rang as they went in and the lady behind the counter smiled, and Alec walked up to her in his slow steady way.

"Alec, a fine morning, isn't it?" she said in a brisk tone and then turned to Penny and smiled.

"Ellen this is Penny she is staying at The Lookout," he said with a slight sniff. Ellen was quite round and she had short red hair, and electric blue eyes and was probably in her early forties.

"Well welcome to the Island, what's your name again?" she said smiling

"Penny," said Alec.

"Right the lassie needs some things," Alec rested his

hands on the counter and looked up at Ellen. Alec then started to speak in a weird language, which Penny guessed was Gaelic. Ellen just nodded and now again would say "aye".

Penny looked and picked up a basket and walked around the shop, taking items from the dusty shelves. She would wince every time she picked something up and would wipe her hand down her jeans.

"This is certainly not my type of store," she sighed to herself.

Penny noticed Alec and Ellen watching her. She confidently walked over to the counter and placed her basket down. Alec leaned into Penny "Don't you need some bits?" he said.

"Yes, I have some bits here," Penny looked down at him and showed him the contents of her basket.

"No, he means shoes," said Ellen, laughing at Penny.

"I have a lovely pair of boots come in. What size are you?" she said bending down and rummaging through a box under the counter.

"Five," Penny peered over.

"You are in luck, here we go," she stood up and opened the long box and took out some yellow wellingtons.

"Do you have anything a little less bright?" said Alec almost squinting at the brightness.

"It's either these or you will have to go over to the mainland," Ellen glared at Alec.

"I will take them; how much are they?" Penny gave Ellen a sweet smile.

"They are a welcoming present," Ellen had a beaming smile and pushed the box towards Penny.

"Are you sure?" Penny whispered.

"Absolutely, now let me get you a bag," and she went under the counter again.

The shop door opened, and the bell rang. Alec and Penny turned around to see Ethan coming through the door. He stopped and looked at them. Ethan nodded to Alec and completely ignored Penny. He was wearing a crisp white shirt and dark denim jeans. He walked over to some shelves by the entrance.

Penny watched Ethan looking at the dusty tin cans, now and again he would look over at them.

Ellen popped up, Alec clutched his chest in fright.

"Morning Ethan," said Ellen slightly out of breath and started to run the shopping through the till. Penny felt Ethan come up behind them. Penny wanted to look at him, but he had been so rude, she stood with her back to him.

"Right, that will be five pounds and twenty pence," said Ellen holding out her hand.

Penny opened her bag, trying to look for her purse. She was rummaging around. Ethan gave a frustrated sigh. Penny, tensed up, and looked over her shoulder at him. He gave a quick smile. She eventually found it and gave Ellen the money. Penny picked up her shopping and turned around. Ethan moved to the side to let her pass. Penny hadn't realised how tall Ethan was.

Penny hurried to the door and then Ellen shrieked "The boots!"

Penny slowly turned around and walked back up to the counter, not making any eye contact with Ethan. She smiled at Ellen and picked up the box and placed it under her arm. As she turned around the wellington's fell out of the box.

"Butterfingers," Ethan whispered; Penny bent down to pick them up.

"Ethan, where are your manners?" Ellen hissed.

"Sorry," and he moved away from Penny, so she could pick up the wellingtons. Penny looked up at him and scowled.

"Ethan," said Ellen crossly and hit the counter.

He reluctantly bent down and helped Penny put the wellingtons in the box and they both stood up at the same time. Penny could not look at him and pretended to check her bag.

"Thank you," Penny whispered looking at the floor.

As she reached the door, she heard Ethan say, "Bye then." His tone sarcastic.

Penny turned to look at him and he gave a strained smile. Penny scowled at him; his rude behaviour was becoming unacceptable.

Once outside and the door had shut, Penny turned to Alec.

"What is wrong with him? He is so…"Penny said through gritted teeth, looking back at the shop.

Alec slowly shuffled towards his car and opened his door and eased himself in, and leaned over to open the passenger door. Penny opened the door and threw the shopping in the back seat and sat down and wedged the box in between her legs. She put her seatbelt on, and Alec started the engine.

"Alec, why is Ethan so rude?" Penny huffed folding her arms.

"If you knew, you would understand," he turned the key and the car shuddered and they drove off.

They sat in silence speeding down the road, the shopping sliding around in the back seat. Penny looked out of the window, the fields whizzing past, the landscape changed from hilly, to flat marshland and then to high cliffs. Alec started to slow down as they approached the cottage. He pulled up on the side of the road and Penny got out. She leant in the back and collected her shopping which was now all over the seat and in the footwell.

"Thank you, Alec and I guess I will see you around?" Penny felt uneasy, that now she would be on her own.

"Lassie if you need anything, you know where I am." He said trying to smile and drove back to his cottage.

Penny took a deep breath and walked up the white dusty path. She kicked the pot over and picked up the key, opened the door and stood in the doorway. The breeze from outside came flooding into the room. The silence was unbearable, and Penny's emotions began to well up inside her. She threw her bag onto the sofa and crumpled to the floor.

"How did it get so bad?" she screamed and hit the ground with her fists. Eventually, she pulled herself together and wearily stood up and looked around. The first thing she needed to do was to make it homely, and tomorrow when she got the hire car, she would go back to Ellen's and buy some things to cheer the place up.

Exploring the cottage, took five minutes. The bathroom was small and very dated and looking around Penny realised that there were no radiators. So, there was no central heating.

Penny opened the front door, hanging on the back, was an old yellow raincoat. She put it on, took the key and went to search for a coal shed or woodpile. There was a small shed at the far end of the garden. She opened the door, and a bird flew out, Penny screamed and held her chest in fright. She heard someone laughing and quickly turned around. Ethan had his arms folded and was clutching a plastic bag.

"Are you following me?" Penny sniped.

"No, Ellen asked me to drop these off for you," he held out the bag at arm's length and shook it.

"Right, I see, thank you," Penny took a step closer to him and took the bag from him.

They stood in silence; Penny found herself gazing at Ethan. His aviator glasses flashed in the sunlight. He had an air of arrogance, though at the same time, slight vulnerability. He was difficult to work out.

"See you around then," Ethan eventually said.

He turned and walked away; Penny stood clutching the bag.

"Ethan wait,"

Penny followed him down the path almost tripping on a rock.

He stopped and turned to wait for Penny.

"I feel we have got off on the wrong foot, so can we start

again?" holding her hand out.

He shook her hand limply.

"See you," he said, and he walked off.

She watched him get into his car, it started to cloud over, and the wind suddenly whipped up. The door of the shed was violently blowing back and forth in the wind.

Penny walked back to the shed and in the back was a bag of coal. She dragged it out and pulled it into the cottage. Penny remembered the bag which Ethan had dropped off. The rain was heavy, and the wind was blowing.

"Really?" Penny hurried outside and picked up the bag.

She ran back into the cottage and wiped the rain off her face and attempted to make the fire. She knelt, by the fire and piece by piece dropped the lumps of coal into the fire basket.

"Where are the matches?" she moaned, hitting the floor with her hand.

She looked in the cupboards, and the kitchen, there were no matches. Penny sat down on the chair in despair and put her head in her hands and said over and over "You can do this, just keep going."

Penny quickly stood up and out of frustration kicked the bag Ethan had brought over. All the contents flew across the floor.

Penny felt that all her Christmases had come at once. Scattered across the floor were fire-lighters, matches, basically a survival kit. Ellen was her guardian angel, Penny started to cry with joy.

Ellen had written a note.

Just pay me back when you are next in, Ellen MacDonald xx

Eventually, Penny got the fire going, it smoked a lot, but she did not care and was glad for the warmth. Exhausted, Penny collapsed on the sofa bed and fell into a deep sleep.

When Penny eventually awoke, it had gone past nine-thirty, it was twilight, the sound of the sea even more intense outside. She heard a car drive past, the lights of the car lit up the ceiling above her.

She lay for a while, staring at the front door. The fire had almost gone out. Penny turned the sidelight on and got the fire going, closed the curtains and went to make some dinner. The loneliness was setting in and she sat at the table wondering how she would ever get out of this situation. The only thing that was getting Penny through this was, that as soon as the date for the court case had been set, she would be leaving this island. Penny stood up and went over to the electric hob and waited for the rings to go orange. She found a rusty pot and poured the soup into the bowl and went over to her suitcase and opened it. Penny had packed the most ridiculous items, she did however pack a warmish jumper and put that on. The smell of damp wafting around the cottage was becoming unbearable. She squirted some perfume in the air and the heat of the fire was starting to warm up the cottage.

Suddenly there was a knock at the door. Penny froze and was in two minds about opening it. Penny crept over to the fireplace and picked up the poker and slowly walked over to the door and stood listening, she could hear shuffling.

"Penny it's Alec," he said nervously.

Penny let out a sigh of relief and opened the door.

"Alec, you scared the living daylights out of me," laying the poker down.

Alec stood with a radio.

"Come in," Penny beckoned.

He shuffled in and went to sit down on the chair.

"Sorry if I scared you, but I was on my way out and I thought I would drop this off for you," he said placing the radio on the table.

"I thought you might like this. It's not one of those fancy ones, but it works, and you can pick up a station…just."

"Thank you, Alec," Penny watched him shuffle over to the front door.

"Well, night then," he said and opened the door.

"Night Alec," and he slowly walked to his car which was parked on the verge.

Even though he was a cantankerous old man, at least Alec was company. Penny closed the door and could smell her soup now burning on the stove. Penny scraped the contents into the bowl and forced herself to eat her soup. She plugged the radio in and frantically turned the dials and moved the aerial and eventually found a local station, in Gaelic. She turned it off.

The next morning, Penny awoke to a knock at the door. Startled and not knowing where she was, she leapt from the sofa bed and frantically looked around the room.

"Who is it?" Penny walked towards the front door.

"Caledonian Motors, I have your hire car," said a man.

Penny opened the door, and the man was standing with a clipboard.

"If you wouldn't mind signing here," he said pointing at the page. Penny took the clipboard and remembered to sign her name as Penny Hargreaves.

She handed it back to him and he gave her the keys. The man then turned around and walked to another car parked further along the verge.

"Hey, don't I have to check things over with you?" Penny shouted.

"No bother, I trust you," he said and got into the other car and drove off.

Penny stood there for a while with the keys in her hand. She stepped out of the cottage and there parked on the verge was a small red Fiat Uno. It must have been over twenty years old, Penny felt so deflated.

Penny went back into the cottage and decided to have a shower. The bathroom was cold and damp. She turned on the shower, which was above the bath. Suddenly, brown water started to come out and then it made a gurgling sound. She looked down and there was mud floating around. She turned off the shower and turned the bath taps on and the mud washed out and thankfully the water was clear. Penny eased herself into the bath and the water was warm, not hot but it would do. She lay there staring up at the ceiling, which had yellow stains on it, mould all over the walls. The bathroom was a faded pink colour, old wallpaper could be seen underneath the paint.

After her bath, Penny made a coffee and went outside and there was a small bench at the end of the path leading to the road. Penny went to sit down. It was so quiet, only the sound of the sea and seagulls flying around. The sea was a brilliant blue and the sand white. The sun was warm,

Penny began to relax a little. She looked at the beach and saw a man running along the sand. As the person got closer, she saw it was Ethan. He was wearing blue tracksuit bottoms and a white t-shirt. Penny watched him run further down the beach, he then vanished around a bend. Ethan intrigued her, he was not her type, though he had something about him, he just got under her skin.

Penny sat there for a little longer and finished her coffee and decided to go back to Ellen's to get more items. She picked up her bag and coat and decided to wear her new wellingtons, as the high heels were just not practical. The last time Penny wore wellingtons was in Glastonbury last Summer. She unlocked the car and an air of stale cigarette smoke wafted out. She got in and started the engine and the car was shuddering. It then stalled. The car did not turn over. Penny was miles away and did not notice Alec walk up to the car. He knocked on the window.

"You need to pull out the choke," his voice muffled.

Penny wound down the window.

"I need to do what?" Penny asked.

"The choke, down there on your left under the steering wheel," he leant in pointing at a leaver.

"What?" Penny gripped the steering wheel and looked down.

"Turn on your engine," Alec leaned further in.

Penny winced; Alec smelt awful. She noticed that he had dribbled his breakfast down his shirt.

Penny turned the key "Now what?"

"Slowly pull it out," he said in a calm tone.

Penny pulled the choke out and it stalled again.

"No slowly, you don't want to flood the engine?" he said now annoyed.

Penny glared at him and turned on the engine and gently pulled out the choke.

"That's it... now you feel it pulling, now raise the clutch," he said smiling and tapped her shoulder.

Penny squealed in delight.

"Do you want a lift, Alec?" Penny trying to be grateful but feeling a complete fool.

"No lassie, I will be getting on, just wanted to check all was ok," he was now smiling.

"Right see you later," Penny smiled at him and he nodded and walked down the path.

Penny pulled out and nervously drove down the road, admiring the view and wasn't paying attention, she looked in her rear-view mirror and blue flashing lights were behind her. She panicked and almost drove off the road, the police car was coming fast behind her. She slowed down and turned into a parking bay at the side of the road. The police car, which was a Defender Land Rover, pulled- in behind her.

"Why me, why me?" Penny squealed.

The driver's door of the police car opened, and a policeman got out and put on his cap, he was wearing sunglasses. The policeman bent down. Penny wound the window down and looked up, it was Ethan.

"Hello Ethan," Penny said, a rush of excitement transcended through her body, at Ethan in his uniform.

"Sergeant Mackenzie to you. Do you know how fast you were going back there?" he said standing up and looking down the road.

"No," Penny said slightly flustered.

"Fifty-five" he took out a pad from his back pocket.

"Listen Ethan," he gave her a disapproving look.

"Sorry, Sergeant Mackenzie, I promise I won't do it again, I was just getting used to the car," she said stroking the steering wheel with her hand.

"I guess it is more paperwork for me," he said tapping the pad now on the top of the car roof.

"Exactly," Penny smiled and looked up at him.

"But I am still going to give you a ticket, rules are rules," he wrote out the ticket and handed it to her.

"Hey, this is not fair," Penny protested snatching the ticket from him.

"Don't get me started on your brake lights, pay the fine and get your lights fixed." He said crossly and walked back to his car.

Penny looked in the rear-view mirror, Ethan sat looking at Penny. She didn't want him to follow her, so she waited for him to go first. Eventually, he started the engine, as he was passing her, he slowed down a little and shook his head at her and then sped up.

"Rules are rules," Penny mimicked Ethan and scrunched up the ticket and threw it in the back seat.

After five minutes, Penny had the car going, she took a few wrong turns but eventually arrived in the town. She parked opposite Ellen's shop. It was a pretty town, some of the buildings were painted bright colours, and there was a quayside, butchers, fishmongers, and Ellen's shop. A ferry was leaving the port and Penny wished she was on the ferry, though something was stopping her from escaping.

Penny opened the door to the shop and the bell rang above her and Ellen popped up from below the counter. She was eating a cake and nervously wiped her lips.

"Oh, you caught me," she said giggling, sounding like Mrs Doubtfire.

"Ellen thank you so much for the bag of goodies yesterday," Penny placed her handbag on the counter.

"Oh, I can't take the credit," she said smiling and wiping her hands on her dress.

Penny gave her a puzzled look.

"It was Ethan's idea," she said her eyes twinkling.

"Ethan…" Penny whispered and raised her eyebrows.

"Yes, Ethan," she said giving Penny a wink.

"Right," Penny gave a strained smile.

"Now what can I do for you?" Ellen said resting her hands on the counter and wiping some cake from her hands in the process.

"I just need a few more things, is it ok if I have a browse?"

"Of course, take your time, I am just going to go in the back, yell if you need me," Ellen said and walked through a doorway.

Penny walked up and down the aisle looking at the shelves crammed with items and went around the corner.

She stood behind a shelf.

"So, tell me Penny why have you come to live on the island?" Asked Ellen, who sounded like she was lifting a heavy box.

Penny took a deep breath before answering.

"I am a journalist doing some research on island life," hoping she sounded convincing and stayed behind the shelf.

The bell rang above the door, and Penny heard someone walk into the shop.

"Tell me Ellen what's Ethan's story, why is he so rude and arrogant?" Penny shouted picking up some rather ugly looking ornaments.

There was complete silence.

"Ellen are you there?" Penny peered around the shelf and standing at the counter was Ethan. Ellen looked down at the floor.

"Sergeant Mackenzie," Penny said walking past him and wincing with embarrassment.

He stormed out of the shop. Penny turned and looked at Ellen "Whoops…"

"He we will be fine," said Ellen trying to make light of the situation, waving her hand around.

"Seriously why is he so rude and standoffish?" Penny leant on the counter.

"It's not really my place to say," Ellen nervously picked up an object from the counter and polished it with a duster.

"I should go and find him and apologise," Penny bit her bottom lip.

"Penny please leave it," Ellen whispered, her face full of worry.

"Fine, next time I see him," Penny gave Ellen a nervous smile.

"Changing the subject completely; next Saturday, there is a ceilidh here, in the town. You will get a real sense of island life there… for your book," Ellen said with excitement.

"Ceilidh?" Penny frowned, then quickly realised that it might look strange if she did not know what a ceilidh was.

"Oh, a ceilidh," Penny said still none the wiser.

"So, will you come?" Ellen said gleefully.

"Yes, why not, as you said, good research," Penny walked back to the shelves.

"Penny, can I ask you a personal question?" Ellen lowering her voice.

Penny slowly turned around and wondered if she had blown her cover.

"Sorry ignore me," Ellen said waving her hand and turning away with embarrassment.

"No go on Ellen," Penny now curious.

"I noticed you were not wearing a wedding ring and therefore are you single?" she asked nervously.

Penny cleared her throat "Hmmm… yes guilty thirty-five and not married, yep Bridget Jones me… though I have just come out of a relationship," Penny feeling now rather uncomfortable.

"With a man?" Ellen blurted out.

"Yes, with a man..." Penny was taken aback.

"So sorry, I didn't mean to say that out loud, sorry if I offended you," Ellen looked down at the floor, embarrassed, her cheeks crimson.

"Ellen, you haven't..." Penny gave a gentle smile.

"Right, I will let you get on, just yell if you need me," Ellen darted through to the back.

Penny got a few items and came back to the counter.

"Ellen, I have got everything," Penny called out.

Ellen came out, she made no eye contact with Penny.

"Can I just say sorry again and can I explain?" She was slightly out of breath.

"Honestly, there is no need," Penny trying to reassure Ellen.

"Ethan is my cousin, and he has had a rough time of it lately and I just want Ethan to be happy." Ellen was trying to smile.

"Ethan is your cousin?" It was now all falling into place for Penny.

Ellen nodded her head nervously and ran her finger along the counter.

"Right let me price these up," Ellen grabbed the basket from Penny and ran the items through.

"Ok, that will be fifteen pounds exactly," she said.

"Oh, how much do I owe you for yesterday?" Penny looked in her purse for more money, she was running low on cash. Ellen only took cash.

"It's fine, honestly," Ellen said pushing the purse away.

"Ellen please…" Penny sighed.

"Ethan paid, just now that's why he was here," Ellen looked down at the counter.

"Well, I will thank him when I next see him and apologise, though it might help me if you fill me in on why he acts all …well you know," Penny leant against the counter.

"All I can say is that Ethan has had a very hard couple of years," Ellen said looking extremely sad.

"Fine I will go easy on him then and I will see you next week at the Wayleigh," Penny said excitedly

"C…ceilidh," Ellen said smiling.

CHAPTER 3

Penny drove back to the cottage and again the loneliness hit her when she walked through the door. She put the bag down and unpacked the items she had bought, which consisted of a tartan rug, a vase, and a cushion with a deer on it. Penny went into the kitchen and put the kettle on. There was a small window above the sink, and on the coal shed, there was a cat. Desperate for company Penny went outside and tried to coax the cat to come and say hello. It eventually jumped down and walked slowly towards her. He was a tabby and came up to her legs and started to rub his head on her wellingtons. Penny stroked his head and the cat started to purr. Penny went back inside, and the cat followed.

Penny did not care if he belonged to someone, he jumped up on the sofa and then curled up and fell asleep.

By six o'clock she was starting to get cabin fever. When she was driving into town this morning, she noticed a pub. Penny needed to be around people and decided if she had to act the part of a journalist, she should sit in the pub writing something and having a drink. Wellingtons were too much and put her high heels back on and some makeup. She was still getting used to her hair colour and thought, she needed a complete change. Penny went to the drawer in the kitchen and found a pair of scissors, walked back to the fireplace, stood in front of the mirror, and slowly chopped her hair into a long bob. She turned around to the cat and said, "What do you think?"

The cat blinked in agreement.

Penny drove to the pub, thrilled to be out of her cottage. The pub was on a cliff just outside the town. It had wonderful panoramic views of the island. When Penny arrived, the sun was setting, and the orange sun gave the pub a pink glow. It had distinctive whitewash walls, and the windows were painted a soft sage green. Hanging baskets hung at the entrance and gently swung in the sea breeze. A white chalky path led up to the pub entrance, on either side wildflowers grew. The pub was called the Ship Inn, and to Penny it was heaven.

Penny opened the heavy oak door; it groaned as she did so. She walked into a tiny porch; she could hear the murmur of people talking on the other side of the connecting door. She opened the door, to the bar and was greeted by a strong smell of beer and the loos. The table and chairs were old and tattered. It was dark and dingy and everyone in the pub was over sixty and all men. The pub fell silent when Penny walked in and they all turned to look at her. The landlord had white silver hair and was in his early fifties, with tattoos all over his arms and a noticeable scar on his face. He frowned when he saw Penny and folded his arms. Penny walked to the bar and was feeling the hostility in the room. When she reached the bar, he leant down and whispered.

"Listen probably best you don't stay around," he said in a strong Glaswegian accent.

"Why?" Penny looked directly at the landlord and placed her bag on the bar.

"Jimmy let her come in, she is with me," said a voice from the corner of the room. Penny turned around; Alec was sitting at a small round table. She gave Alec a warm smile and picked up her bag, which was damp with beer from the bar and walked over to him.

"May I?" Penny quietly asked Alec.

"Aye," the pub started to talk again. He leaned back in his chair and tilted his head.

"What?" Penny feeling self-conscious.

Alec pointed to her hair and gave her a wink; she smiled in embarrassment.

"Alec, why did the Landlord tell me to leave?" Penny took off her yellow coat and placed it on the back of her chair and turned around and glared at the landlord.

"If you hadn't noticed lassie, there are only men in here," he said downing his whisky.

"Let me get you another one," Penny jumped up and walked to the bar.

"Can I have two of whatever he is having?" Penny pointed at Alec.

"Your money is not good in here," said the Landlord sighing and began to clean a glass, with a stained tea towel.

"Why?" Penny sighed and picked up a beer mat and tapped it on the bar.

Jimmy did not answer and walked to the other side of the bar to serve an old man.

"Charming," Penny said under her breath.

"Jimmy, show some respect to the lassie," said Alec firmly.

Jimmy finished serving the old man and slowly went to pour out the drinks and slammed them down. Penny took the glasses and moved away from the bar.

"Hey missy, are you not forgetting something?" Jimmy draped the tea towel over his shoulder.

Penny slowly turned around "You said my money was not good in here," giving him a sarcastic smile.

"And this is why women are not allowed in here," said an old man sitting on a barstool.

"It's 2019, not 1919," Penny growled.

"Penny …pay Jimmy," Alec huffed and shuffled around on his chair.

Penny went over to Alec and placed the drinks down and gave him a look and went to pay Jimmy.

"How much?" Penny now starting to feel uncomfortable, though she was determined not to show any vulnerability to these men.

"Eight pounds," said Jimmy and held out his hand.

"Can I use contactless?" Penny now wished she had stayed at the cottage.

Jimmy shook his head and then sighed. She went through her purse, found the correct money, and went to join Alec.

"Seriously are women not allowed in here?" Penny whispered to Alec.

Alec looked over her shoulder at Jimmy and said "Aye" and sat back in his chair and tapped the side of his glass.

"Wow, I didn't think these places existed anymore," Penny was astounded.

"Penny maybe you should think about staying at home at night," and he gave her a knowing look.

"Alec, I know that you are minding my back and I really appreciate it, I really do. Though I am going stir crazy looking at four walls, besides won't people think it's odd that I spend most of the time on my own, considering I am meant to be a journalist writing about these islands," Penny hissed.

Alec did not answer and calmly sipped his whisky. Penny took a sip of her drink and coughed loudly. It was like firewater.

"I might just get myself some water and a wine, here have mine," and pushed the glass towards Alec, still coughing, her eyes streaming.

Penny walked up to the bar.

"Babycham?" said Jimmy almost laughing and leant down to her, his blue eyes twinkling.

"Jimmy," Alec growled.

"Sorry, what would Madam like?" Jimmy gave Alec a stern look.

"White wine... large please," Penny smiled sweetly at him.

"Of course," he gave a strained smile.

The door to the pub opened a group of young men came in, they were rather loud and when they saw Penny, they all stopped talking. The group of men were in their early twenties and looked like trouble. Shaven hair, Ben Sherman shirts and jeans.

"Here we go," Alec mumbled and looked at his empty

glass.

"I think I have died and gone to heaven," said one of them and came to sit in between Alec and Penny. He had Love tattooed on the top of his right hand.

"What's your name?" he said looking at Penny, furiously chewing gum.

"Please leave," said Alec not looking at the man.

"No, grandpa," he grabbed Penny's hand, and she quickly pulled it away.

"Hey, no trouble," said Jimmy coming from around the bar. The man stood up and walked to the bar and put his hands up and gave a menacing smile.

"No, bother, I promise," and slapped Jimmy on the arm and went over to join his friends. The young men all congregated at the bar and were whispering and then laughing and turning around, looking at Penny.

"Penny it might be best if you leave," said Alec whispering and genuinely looking concerned for her safety.

"No, Alec I am not going because of them," Penny took a sip of her wine and made no eye contact with the young men. She had dealt with worse.

One of the men walked over to the jukebox and put some music on. The man who had originally come over to Penny and Alec called from the bar.

"Would you like a dance?" and turned back to his friends laughing.

Penny ignored them and looked nervously at Alec who was now shaking his head in annoyance at the men's behaviour.

"Hey, I said do you want to dance?" he said aggressively and walked over to Penny. Alec stood up slowly, as if to protect Penny. The man pushed him down to his seat.

"How dare you," Penny said crossly and stood up and gave him a slight push. The man feeling slightly emasculated by Penny came closer to her and rested his hands on her shoulders and gave a wicked smile.

The pub door opened, and in walked Ethan, he was looking at his phone, he briefly looked up from his phone and scanned the room. He nodded at Jimmy, who was now coming around from the bar.

"Lads let's move outside," said Ethan gesturing they left.

"No," said the man and walked up to Ethan, his friends made a circle around Ethan.

Ethan looked at Jimmy and took a deep breath and walked up to the man and grabbed him by his shoulders and pushed him towards the door. The man took a swing, Ethan ducked and then grabbed his shoulders and spun him around and had him in a half nelson. From his back pocket, Ethan produced his warrant card and held it in front of the man's face.

"I am Sergeant Mackenzie, and I am asking you and your friends to leave." Hissed Ethan.

The men scared by Ethan suddenly rushed out of the pub. The man nodded and Ethan let go. The man slowly walked to the door, when he got to the door, he rolled his shoulders, turned, and went for Ethan. In one fell swoop, Ethan had the man on the floor.

"Now leave" whispered Ethan standing above him and holding his hand out, to help him up. The man slowly got up and walked out, slamming the door.

Ethan put his warrant card in his back pocket and when he saw Penny, he raised his eyebrows at her and walked to the bar.

"The usual Ethan?" Asked Jimmy turning his back to him and taking down a bottle of whisky from the shelf and pouring him his drink. Ethan got out his wallet from his back pocket and Jimmy put his hand out and shook his head. Ethan gave him a nod and went to sit down at a table in the corner of the pub. Ethan grabbed a newspaper from one of the other tables and sat down and was staring into space, Penny watched him intensely.

"Lassie it is rude to stare" Alec whispered.

Penny quickly turned around and smiled at Alec.

"Alec, I just need to talk to Ethan." Penny nervously walked over to Ethan who was now looking down at his phone. She cleared her throat "Ethan can I have a word?"

He looked up and put his phone in his pocket.

"Ethan please" Penny was fidgeting.

"Yes, what is it?" He sat upright and stretched upwards and looked over at Jimmy.

"Well, a couple of things" Penny sat down and nervously tapped the table with her fingers.

"Firstly, can I apologise for this morning, secondly, thank you for buying the supplies for me, and thirdly thank you for just now," Penny quickly stood up.

"Apology excepted for this morning," he looked away from her.

"Well thank you again," Penny slowly turned around to go

back to sit with Alec.

"Penny…" Ethan called out.

Penny turned around to look at him. His eyes intensely looked at her.

"I hope you are not driving home?" he leaned forward and pointed at the window.

She gave him a puzzled look.

"Lights…" and sat back in his seat.

"No…" Penny quietly said and went to sit down with Alec.

"Think you have made a friend there," Alec nodded at Ethan and downed his whisky.

Penny turned around and looked at Ethan, he was now swiping through his phone.

"Penny, we need to go, I will drive you home, we do not want Ethan to chastise you anymore," Alec slowly stood up.

"Thank you," Penny whispered and picked her bag up.

She waited for Alec to catch up with her. Penny stepped backwards and did not realise Ethan was now standing behind her. She quickly turned around and they bumped into each other. Ethan stood back from her and opened the door for her, smiling. Penny walked through and he let the door close on her and she heard laughter from inside the pub.

Tears welled up in her eyes, she looked back at the pub. Tomorrow she was leaving this ghastly island.

CHAPTER 4

They arrived back at the cottage and Alec dropped Penny off. She walked up to the front door and got the keys out of her bag. A car pulled up on the grass verge. Penny quickly put the key in the door and hurried in. She turned the main light on and as she was closing the curtains, she saw someone walking up the path. She needed to get a security light; she could not see who it was. There was a knock at the door.

Penny looked over to the sofa, the cat was still asleep.

"Why couldn't you have been a dog," Penny hissed.

There was another knock.

"Penny it is Ethan," Penny gave a huge sigh of relief and opened the door.

"You forgot this," he shoved her yellow coat into her hand.

"Thank you, Ethan," Penny gave a quick smile.

"Well, night then," as Ethan turned to leave, the cat came and stood by her feet.

"Hey, that's my son's cat," Ethan bent down and picked the cat up.

"Sorry he just came into the house this morning; I

didn't realise that he belonged to anyone," Penny gave an apologetic smile.

"He is she," Ethan said curtly holding the cat tightly. Penny rolled her eyes at Ethan.

The cat scrambled to get down and jumped to the floor and walked over to the sofa.

"She loves you," Penny said laughing.

Ethan gave a smile.

"Well just for tonight she can stay, though my life won't be worth living if she is not home tomorrow for breakfast," He sighed

Ethan turned around and walked down the path.

"What's her name?" Penny shouted.

"Queenie…" he shouted back not looking at Penny and waved his hand in the air.

"Bye then…" Penny quietly said to herself and closed the door.

Penny walked over to the sofa and sat down, and the cat jumped up onto her lap.

"Why is your daddy so angry?" Penny rubbed the cat's head and lay back on the sofa. Ethan was a mystery.

Penny awoke to the cat pawing at her. She slowly sat up and saw that it was six o'clock in the morning.

"Right Queenie, you need to go home," Penny opened the front door and shooed her away. The cat did not move.

"Please yourself," Penny walked into the kitchen; the cat followed her in.

"Queenie go…" Penny pointed at the door.

The cat flicked her tail as if to say no. Penny closed the front door and realised that there was no lock on the inside, her security was becoming a serious issue.

Penny went for a shower, hoping there would be no leaves or twigs this time. After her lukewarm shower, Penny dressed and decided to go for a walk.

Penny stepped outside the cottage, and Queenie quickly ran out of the door, following Penny across the road onto the beach. It was a grey day, but the light was amazing, it had a silver-blue hue, and the sun was trying to break through the clouds. Penny walked along the empty beach deep in thought.

"Hello Penny," said a voice, Penny turned to her side, and saw Ethan run past. He carried on running and then stopped and bent over and slowly stood up with his hands on his hips.

"See you are still a cat thief," he said, his eyes sparkling. Ethan had a soft Scottish accent, not harsh like Alec.

Penny looked down and Queenie was still following her, like a shadow. Ethan then clapped his hands at Queenie, and she ran off towards the road.

"Hey, that's not fair, I can't help it if she likes me," Penny was almost smiling.

"You don't strike me as one of those mad women with a hundred cats," said Ethan his face alive now.

"What type am I then?" Penny said in a flirty tone.

"The princess type…" he gave a cheeky smile and sprinted off. Her attraction to Ethan was quickly fading.

Ethan came running back.

"Sorry," he called out running towards her.

"For what?" Penny looked directly ahead, ignoring him.

"Sorry for what I have just said..." he walked beside Penny.

"Ethan, it's probably best if you and I keep our distance, we seem to rub each other up the wrong way," Penny quickened her pace.

He stopped in his tracks and Penny carried on walking.

"You look like a duck in those boots," he shouted.

Penny stopped and turned around; Ethan was now running on the spot.

"Is that the best you can come up with?" Penny shouted trying not to laugh. He smiled to himself and then ran in the other direction.

Penny watched Ethan sprinting off. Even though Ethan was rude most of the time, Penny was slowly becoming attracted to him.

Penny turned back to the cottage and decided to explore the island. Her car was at the pub, so she walked down to Alec's cottage, to see if he would give her a lift to collect it. Penny stood outside his cottage and hesitated before knocking. Maybe she was relying on him too much. She was about to walk back down the track and Alec opened the door.

"Oh, it's you" he came out and closed the door quickly as if he were hiding something.

"Alec, it doesn't matter..." Penny walked off.

"Do you need to collect your car?" he said gruffly.

"Yes, that would be lovely, could you run me to the pub? "Penny pleaded with her hands.

"Ok wait there," he slammed the door.

He was some time and then came back out and walked to his car.

Alec raced along the coastal road. Penny looked over at him.

"In a rush Alec?" Penny said smiling at him.

"Aye," he said showing no emotion.

He stopped by her car, the engine was still running, Penny got out and closed the door and he sped off. A cloud of dust covered Penny; she fanned it away.

"Bye then..." she whispered and got into her car.

Driving down the road she tried to work out why Alec had changed, she put it down to him just having a bad day and didn't give him a second thought.

The island was tiny, Penny had driven around the island in forty-five minutes, twice. Penny ended up on the headland and there was a kiosk selling drinks and a group of cyclists gathered in a car park.

Penny drove into the car park and sat looking out to sea. She could just make out the mainland and all the fear came flooding back. Penny had only been here a couple of days and the idea of staying on the island for longer than a month made her depressed again.

Penny spied a large woman with a young boy, it was Ellen. Penny got out and called her name. She turned around and did not respond. Penny waved again and called her name. Ellen walked towards Penny, the little boy running behind her.

"Oh, Penny it's you, "Ellen said laughing and quickening

her pace.

"I didn't recognise you, your hair is different," she said smiling.

"Yes, fancied a change," Penny smiled down at the little boy.

"Hello, and who are you?" Penny said bending down to the little boy.

"This is Sammy, Ethan's son," said Ellen smiling. The boy had Ethan's jet-black hair though it was curly and freckles on his face.

"Hello Sammy, I met Queenie yesterday," Penny said warmly.

Sammy nervously looked away.

"Don't be shy Sammy?" said Ellen a little embarrassed by his reaction and pulled him close to her.

"Ethan with you?" Penny looked at the cyclists who passed them.

"No, he is working so I am babysitting Sammy," she said sighing.

"Right Ellen, I will let you get on and I will see you soon, no doubt," Penny turned to walk away.

"Oh Penny, I have been a complete fool," Ellen said grabbing Sammy and walking up to Penny.

"The Ceilidh is this Saturday night," she said with a strained smile.

"As tonight Saturday?" Penny stood back from Ellen.

"Aye," she said "Can you still come? It will be a hoot, I am going," her eyes smiling.

"Ellen I am not exactly flooded with engagements, so yes why not, we can have a girl's night!"

"Great, well make sure you get your drinking boots on, I will come to yours for around seven if that's ok?" tapping Penny's arm. Penny nodded and waved goodbye and went back to her car. Secretly she hoped Ethan would be there. Though no doubt with his gorgeous wife, she felt depressed again.

Penny drove back to the cottage and spent most of the day pottering around. She tied a washing line in the garden, unearthed a lot of pots behind the coal shed and on Monday, she would go into town and buy some flowers to brighten up the garden. She also found a windchime on the floor and it was still intact, so hung it on the small tree that was in the garden. Penny looked at the time it was six o'clock. She quickly rummaged through the small number of clothes, and she only had the jeans and a semi-smart top and again her high heels. It would have to do. She put some makeup on and sat on the sofa waiting for Ellen to arrive.

Ellen arrived at seven, Penny opened the door.

Ellen hesitated.

"Come in Ellen...don't be shy."

Ellen was wearing a kilt and was looking quite smart, she held up a plastic bag.

"I hope you don't mind, but I didn't think you would have a kilt, so here you are," and thrust the bag into Penny's hand.

"That is so sweet of you, I will just go and get change," Penny pointed at the bathroom.

Penny shouted, "Make yourself at home," as she hurried into the bathroom.

Penny opened the bag, and there was a woollen skirt, it looked like something her grandmother used to wear to church on Christmas day.

"There are some tights in there too, it gets a wee nippy in the hall, but after a few drams you won't feel the cold," Ellen shouted and then went quiet.

Penny came out and Ellen was perched on the sofa, clutching her knees with her hands.

"Right... let me just get my bag and we can go," Penny turned off the sidelight and let Ellen go out first. Penny caught a glimpse of herself in the reflection of the window. She looked hideous.

Penny struggled to close the door of the cottage as a wind had whipped up and blew hard around the cottage. It was still light, and the sky had turned a brilliant red.

"So, where do you live Ellen?" Penny asked, putting her seatbelt on.

"Oh, above the shop. After my divorce it seemed the logical place to make home," she said with a sigh.

"Sorry," Penny looked down at her lap.

Ellen pulled out onto the road and drove extremely slowly, the opposite to Alec.

"Well, no point dwelling..." Ellen gave Penny a quick smile.

Penny could see Ellen was upset by the divorce and got the impression; that it was not her choice.

"So does Ethan's wife work too...because you were with

Sammy this morning?" Penny asked nervously and was annoyed with herself she had asked the question.

Ellen kept her eyes on the road and took a big gulp and cleared her throat "No" she said quietly and completely shut Penny down.

They arrived outside the Village Hall, which was just down by the quayside. Outside the hall, there was the faint sound of a violin playing, the door opened, and a man and woman came out and lit up a cigarette.

They entered the hall; it was soulless. A violinist was playing on the stage and the bright fluorescent lights above glared down.

"Don't worry it will get livelier later, they play the slow stuff for the oldies and then the real music starts…" Ellen said gleefully, sensing Penny's lack of enthusiasm for tonight.

In the corner of the hall, there was a trestle table, which was the bar. Ellen ushered Penny over. Penny took off her coat, she just wanted to leave, it was awful.

Penny nervously looked around the hall and noticed Jimmy the landlord from the pub. He was laughing with a blonde woman. Ellen looked over to Jimmy and Penny could feel Ellen tense up.

Eventually, they were served, Ellen leaned over and asked loudly for two whiskies', a bottle of wine and some crisps. Penny looked over at Jimmy and put two and two together, Jimmy was Ellen's ex-husband.

Jimmy noticed them and walked over, Ellen tensed up even more and looked down at the table.

"Ellen," said Jimmy quietly and gave Penny a strained

smile.

"Jimmy..." Ellen said crisply, still looking down at the table.

"I just thought I would come and say hello," he said softly.

"Hello," Ellen looked away from him.

Penny feeling uncomfortable, moved away from them. She walked to the other side of the hall, and stood against the wall, watching the hall fill up. Penny looked down and an old lady smiled up at her, Penny smiled back and clung onto her coat tightly and was desperate for a drink. Jimmy and Ellen were still arguing. Eventually, Ellen came over to Penny.

"So sorry about that," Ellen said with a heavy sigh.

"Everything ok Ellen?" Penny leant into her and looked over to Jimmy, who now had a face of thunder.

"Well, Jimmy and I need to sort a few things out. He is my ex, we ran the pub and the shop. He has been so difficult, he still thinks the shop is his," she said sighing.

"Look if you want to go, I understand," Penny rested her hand on her shoulder, hoping she would say yes.

"No, it's fine, right let's go and get those drinks," and pulled Penny back to the bar.

Ellen introduced Penny to a couple of people, and then it went dark in the hall, the stage was lit up with flashing lights, and dry ice was wafting through the hall.

"Here we go," Ellen could not contain her excitement and elbowed Penny a little too hard in her ribs.

Penny smiled at her, thinking this is going to be awful.

The band came on and there was an almighty cheer from

the crowd. The music started and everyone quickly got into eight circles around the room. Penny was thrown into the middle of a circle and not knowing what to do she froze. The music became faster, and the circle, circled her. A rather large man grabbed her hands and spun her around in the middle of the circle.

Penny was becoming dizzy, Ellen quickly pushed her over to another man and he started to do a jig, and Penny tried to copy him. When she thought she had got the hang of it, another man came up to her and shouted, "you are going the wrong way," and pushed her in the opposite direction.

Penny felt someone's hands grab her waist from behind and the person held her hand and spun Penny outwards. The lights from the stage were directly in her eyes, and she could not quite make out the person. She moved to the side, and it was Ethan.

She smiled at him and he leant into her and said "I love your granny skirt… very sexy," he winked at her and then flung her to the side and then pulled her back to him and shouted "matches your duck boots," the music suddenly stopped and the room turned around to look at them.

Penny looked away slightly embarrassed and Ethan walked off to the bar. The band started to play again, and Ellen gave Penny a warm smile, clutching her hands together.

Penny was feeling a little overwhelmed, so she went to sit on a chair. She looked over at Ethan, he was chatting with a couple, and he glanced over to her and they locked eyes, and he nervously looked at the ground.

Ellen walked up to Penny with a beaming smile and sat down.

"It is so good seeing Ethan smile again," Ellen sighed.

"Why is that then?" Penny said itching her legs, the woollen skirt was beginning to annoy her.

Ethan walked over to them.

"So is your wife with you?" Penny scratched her legs and looked up at Ethan.

Ethan's face turned white, he looked at Ellen and stormed out of the hall.

Penny turned to Ellen "What did I say?" Penny shocked by Ethan.

Ellen took a deep breath. "Penny, Ethan's wife died two years ago," she quietly said.

"You could have told me," Penny snapped.

"I know, sorry," she said shaking her head and looking down at her hands.

Penny stood up and walked quickly out of the hall. She stood by the doors looking out at the quay, trying to see if she could see Ethan.

He was standing by some iron railings.

"Ethan," Penny called, he ignored her.

Penny walked over to him. The wind was bitterly cold. He kept his back to her, she was about to put her hand on his shoulder but stopped herself.

"Ethan, Ellen never mentioned your wife, I am so sorry. Obviously, if I had known, I wouldn't have said anything," Penny quietly said.

He slowly turned around.

"Ethan, come back inside," Penny hugged herself to keep

warm.

"Thank you, Penny, but I need to be on my own," and he turned away from her again and put his hands on the rail. He was clutching it so hard, that his knuckles turned white.

"Ethan, I don't know the situation and I......" Ethan turned around.

"No Penny you don't know the situation and if you will excuse me, I need to get back home to my son," and pushed past her.

Ellen had come out of the hall carrying Penny's bag and coat.

Ethan stormed past her "thanks a bunch", he was seething. Ellen stopped in her tracks and dropped the coat and bag on the road and went after him. Penny bent down and picked up her belongings and watched Ellen arguing with Ethan. At one point, Ellen hit his arm, and he started to yell at her. Ethan then started to cry, Ellen embraced him rocking him from side to side and patting his back. He eventually stood back from her and wiped the tears from his eyes. He glanced over at Penny and then walked off.

Ellen slowly walked back to Penny.

"Penny, I will drive you home and I will explain in the car," she sighed.

Penny put on her coat and opened the car door and sat down and sighed. The moon was bright, and Penny was mesmerised by the reflection of the moon on the water.

It had been a week since she had witnessed Jason killing that man. Penny cast her mind back, remembering the incident. After Jason had shot the man, Penny who was in the bathroom, ran to the door knocking over some objects on a shelf. She looked down and noticed on the floor, a pair of diamond earrings. She didn't know why, but she grabbed them and left the house in a blind panic. Penny was brought down to earth, with Ellen waving her hand in front of her face.

"You were miles away," Ellen gave a concerned look, she then started to apologise regarding the situation with Ethan, and Penny zoned out. The last week was now just catching up with her. Maybe Penny was being too trusting and needed to start to become more guarded. She decided that from tonight, she would distance herself from Ellen, Ethan, and Alec.

Ellen pulled up outside Penny's cottage.

"Thanks, Ellen, see you sometime?" Penny quickly got out of the car.

"Penny," called Ellen.

Penny turned to look at Ellen.

"Is everything ok? Please do not let Ethan spoil your night. You may not think it, but I think he likes you; he has a lot to work through, but you are a breath of fresh air."

Penny nodded and limply waved Ellen goodbye,

Penny walked up the path, talking to herself "I can't get involved, I will be hopefully leaving the island and going back to London. Starting something with Ethan would be a huge mistake." She told herself. Maybe it was the loneliness, which was making her fall for Ethan.

Penny made something to eat and sat down at the table.

She then quickly got up and took off the kilt, it was itching so much. She sat down again and began to eat her awful dinner. It was a Pot Noodle with a crusty roll. She slurped on the noodles and ate the bread, crumbs falling everywhere. There was a knock at the door. Penny stood up quickly and called out.

"Who is it?" She picked up the poker by the fire.

"Ethan," he said in a forlorn voice.

Penny put the poker down and opened the door. He looked at her and burst into laughter. He could not stop laughing and turned around and bent over double and was holding his stomach. She looked down, she was wearing her tights, her knickers showing and to make matters worse, her jumper was tucked into her tights. She looked hideous.

"Glad I amuse you," Penny left Ethan at the door laughing and ran into the bathroom and put her trousers on and quickly checked her face in the mirror.

Ethan was standing next to the table when she came out and was lifting her Pot Noodle and pulling a face at it.

He quickly spun around "I preferred before," he said trying not to laugh.

"You have cheered up," Penny mumbled, he moved to the side so she could sit down.

"Penny can I just apologise about earlier," he was scratching his head.

"No need, Ethan honestly," she gazed up at him.

He went to sit on the sofa and quickly stood up, as he had sat on her hairbrush. He put it to one side. They both sat in silence the intensity between them was beginning to get too much. Penny stood up and walked to the kitchen.

"Do you want a coffee or tea?" Penny grabbed two mugs from the sideboard.

"Tea," Ethan was trying to make himself comfortable on the sofa.

Penny opened the fridge.

"Oh drat," she exclaimed and slammed the fridge door.

Ethan looked at her.

"No milk…" Penny gave a quick smile.

"Hang on," Ethan stood up and walked out of the cottage. Penny peered around to see Ethan walking down the path.

"Where is he going?" she whispered to herself.

A few minutes later he came back with a bottle of whisky.

"Bought it today and forgot to take it out of the car, lucky us," he smiled warmly and poured the whisky into the mugs.

Ethan handed a mug to Penny "bottoms up" smiling over the top of his mug and he went to sit down.

Penny raised her mug and took a sip and winced.

"So how long have you been a journalist?" he leant forward and placed the mug on the floor.

"After university" she took another sip of her whisky. Penny was awful at lying.

"Hang on, how do you know I am a journalist?" Penny squinted her eyes at him.

"Ellen…" He looked around the room.

"Why write about the Island?" he asked in an inquisitive tone.

"Oh, you know," Penny made no eye contact with him.

"Right," he said not sure how to pursue further with his interrogation.

"You are not really a journalist, are you?" he said slowly.

"Why do you say that?" Penny retorted.

"Well, I see no laptop, no writing materials of any description. It's like you have come up here..." he suddenly stopped and looked down at the floor.

Penny felt she could play dumb or tell the truth.

"Ethan I am tired, and I am not really up to the Spanish Inquisition tonight, can we do this another time?" Penny took another sip of her whisky.

"Fine suit yourself," Ethan held his hands up.

Again, silence fell, Ethan hung his head and was moving his feet in agitation and rubbed his hands along the top of his legs.

He cleared his throat.

"Well partly the reason why I came here, was to ask you to come to my birthday tomorrow night. For some reason, Ellen has taken a shine to you and thought you would like to come," he kept his head low and didn't look at Penny.

"Yes," Penny quickly said. He looked up, surprised by her answer.

"Right good....here is my address, come for six," he was looking for something to write on. Penny got a pen from her bag and grabbed the paper towel next to her and handed it to him. He scribbled it down and handed it back to her.

Penny looked down at the address and then placed it on the table.

"It's not far from here, just turn left and it is about ten minutes," his eyes now alight.

"Ethan, what was the other reason you came here?" Penny said now standing up and slowly walking towards him.

"It doesn't matter," Ethan walked to the door and then he paused before opening it. Penny stood resting against the door. He suddenly pulled Penny to him and kissed her. He stood back; Penny was in shock.

"That was the second reason and judging from your face it was not a good move," he looked embarrassed and went to open the door.

"Ethan..." Penny felt a wave of emotion come over her.

"I get it," Ethan forlornly looked at the floor.

"No Ethan it's just complicated," Penny grabbed his hand.

He looked down and gave her hand a gentle squeeze and rubbed the top of her hand with his thumb.

"See you tomorrow... hopefully?"

"You will," Penny whispered, now wanting to kiss Ethan again.

He slowly took his hand away and opened the door and Penny watched him walk down the path. When he got to the bottom of the path he stopped and turned around.

"Penny, I don't care the reason why you are here..."

CHAPTER 5

Penny closed the door and took a deep breath. She really needed to keep her distance from Ethan. She was trying to convince herself that the only reason she was falling for Ethan was that she was lonely and scared. How could this relationship seriously go anywhere?

Penny was desperate to tell him about her situation, after all, he was a policeman and surely, he would understand.

Penny decided she would go to his birthday and take each day as it came. For all, she knew it could take months for a court date and weirdly, she was starting to enjoy her time on the island, though was it because of Ethan?

Penny tidied away her plate and Pot Noodles and started to get ready for bed. Her thoughts turned to Jason and began to panic. Her greatest fear was that he would not be charged, and he would be released. Or if there was a court case what would happen if he were not found guilty, would she have to go under Witness Protection for the rest of her life?

The next morning, Penny was woken by a howling gale. Alec was right; when it rains it rains. The rain pounding on the windows, the wind whistled down the chimney. Penny made a fire and a coffee and stood at the window watching the spray of the sea blowing over the road. It was going to be a day at home, doing absolutely nothing.

Though at least she had Ethan's birthday to look forward to. Ethan is the opposite of what she would normally go for in a man. Her past relationships have been superficial. Who had the biggest wallet and could give her the best holidays? Ever since she was in her teens, she always went after the bad boys, never the good steady ones. Her sister Annabel on the other hand was sensible. Married, has two children, and lives an extremely comfortable life in Surrey. Annabel has a part-time job as a legal secretary in a firm in Guilford. Her husband Richard is an Accountant and works in the City. Both children are at prep school. Even Penny's parents have given up on the idea that she might get married.

Just like that, the storm stopped and there was a faint glimpse of blue-sky peeping through the clouds on the horizon.

Penny hurriedly dressed in case the weather changed and put on her boots and stepped outside. Her life in London at weekends, was quite regimented, partly because she lived alone. Saturday mornings would be spent at either the gym or going for a run. Then she would do her food shopping online and would meet a friend for lunch or go to an exhibition. In the evenings, it would be dinner with friends or a club.

Penny walked over to the beach and took a deep breath of fresh air. She scanned the beach hoping to see Ethan. Penny followed the beach; she came up to a cliff. The tide was out, so she walked around to the other side of the cliff, she came around the corner into a bay. Wooden steps snaked up the cliff, there was an impressive house set back, with a tall hedge around the perimeter of the property. At the bottom of the steps, a sign said **Private**. A wooden jetty jutted out to the water.

Penny stood looking up at the steep steps and was about to go back when a figure came running down. As the person came closer, she realised it was Ethan. He was wearing jogging bottoms and a thin jumper and a baseball cap. He sprinted down the steps and slowed down when he saw Penny.

"You're a little early," he said shyly.

"Sorry," Penny scrunched up her face, confused.

"This is my house," he rested against the wooden rail.

"Wow this is your house…" Penny trying not to sound too excited.

"Well, it was my father-in-law's," he said walking down the steps.

"I see," Penny didn't move from her spot and the tide started to come in. She could feel herself starting to sink into the sand.

"The tide is coming in, so you should move," Ethan said quite forcefully.

Penny nodded and looked down at her feet, the waves now nearly up to the top of her bright yellow boots. Penny went to lift her boot, but it was stuck. She tried to lift the other foot and had the same problem.

"Come on, it will come up to your shoulders soon," Ethan said with a frustrated tone.

"Ethan I can't…" Penny squealed.

"What do you mean, you can't," he said running backwards from the tide coming in.

"I am stuck…" she flapped her arms.

"Come on, don't muck around, just pull your foot up," He stood further back, the sea was flooding around them.

"Ethan please can you just help me?" Penny stretched her arms to balance herself.

"Seriously, it's not that hard," Ethan shouted at Penny.

The weather changed, the clouds went dark, and the wind raced across the beach.

"Ethan I am not joking; my boots are stuck," She shouted at him, the sea was now up to her waist.

"You really are one, aren't you," Ethan hissed and waded through the waves. Penny began to cry.

"Put your hands on my shoulders," he was trying to keep his balance, the waves crashing around them.

"On the count of three, I am going to pull you up," looking down at Penny.

"One, two, three," he shouted and lifted her up and as he did, Penny lost her balance and pulled him down. She came free from her wellingtons and they both quickly stood up and then fell again, from the sheer force of the waves.

"Get up," he shouted and grabbed Penny and tried to pull her towards the beach.

"I am trying," Penny was trying to hold onto his arm, and he managed to drag Penny to the beach.

"You are nuts," he said out of breath.

"I didn't know I was going to get stuck," Penny shouted at him and hit his arm.

"You might as well come back to the house."

He ushered Penny towards the steps.

Ethan let Penny go first; they began to climb the steps. The wind was violently blowing, Penny stopped and looked down at the sea below.

"Why are you stopping?" said Ethan impatiently looking up at her.

"I get vertigo," she was clutching the handrail.

"Well don't look down," Ethan said and gave her a little shove.

When they reached the top, Penny could now see the house. It was an enormous, double-fronted, Victorian villa, gothic, dark grey stone. There was a huge white gate, with a keypad. Ethan leaned over Penny and punched some numbers into the keypad. The gate made a buzzing noise and Ethan held it open for her. The grass was well-manicured, the path lined with lavender.

"Wow, Ethan, this place is amazing," Penny stopped and looked around.

"My father-in-law worked for one of the big oil companies," he gave a quick smile.

"So, does he live here now?" Penny squinted her eyes as the sun suddenly came out.

"No, he died five years ago, he left it...." he trailed off and didn't look at Penny.

"You are welcome to dry off, or I can run you home, up to you?" Ethan took off his baseball cap and ran his hand through his hair.

"Whatever is easiest, Ethan," Penny gave a nervous smile.

" I should have some dry clothes somewhere, how about

you have a shower you will catch your death," he was now trying to smile.

He knocked on the door, and through the windowpane, an old lady came to the door. She was tall and thin and had an apron on.

"Ethan, why do you always forget your keys?" she trailed off when she saw them both dripping wet.

"Mary this is Penny, she had a slight accident, so she has come to dry off," he said walking past her. Penny hesitated at the door.

"She seems not the only one," said Mary looking at Ethan.

"Come on in Penny, Mary won't bite," Ethan took off his wet jumper, his shoes making a squelching sound as he walked along the hallway.

Penny walked into the long hallway. It was narrow with York stone flooring, a grandfather clock ticking in the corner. There were stag heads mounted on the wall and a few oil paintings hung on the wall going up the staircase.

"Oh, you are the young lass at The Lookout," she gave a strained smile.

"Ethan, I need to have a chat with you," Mary now a little flustered and quickly walked behind him.

"Penny the bathroom is up at the top of the stairs, second door on the right." Ethan, was looking at some post on the side table in the hall, ignoring Mary.

"Thank you," Penny whispered and took off her wet socks.

Mary was now whispering to Ethan and Penny nervously walked up the stairs into the bathroom. Penny closed the door, locked it, and quickly took off her wet clothes and turned the shower on. She got out of the shower and put the towel around her and stood in front of the mirror and whispered, "Can things get any worse?"

She gathered up her wet clothes and gingerly walked out of the bathroom and hovered at the top of the stairs. She crept down the stairs, and Ethan came running up. He stopped when he saw her.

"Mary has found some clothes and shoes for you," He gave a quick smile.

"Fabulous," Penny was firmly holding the towel around her, her wet clothes dripping on the carpet. Penny stood still and Ethan waited for her to come downstairs.

"Are you going to stand there all day?" He tilted his head.

"No," Penny whispered shaking her head and trying to get past him. He let out a sigh and stood up against the wall and she quickly ran down the stairs. Ellen was walking up the hallway and called out to Penny.

"Hello," she bellowed.

"Hi, Ellen," Penny was slightly embarrassed and feeling a draft where she shouldn't.

"You go and get changed, Mary has made some coffee, go and help yourself, I just need to get some party food from the car" Ellen smiled and walked to the front door.

"Ellen where is the kitchen?" Penny's teeth were chattering.

"Oh, silly me, just down the hall, you can't miss it" Ellen pointed down the hall and hurried to the front door.

Penny walked down the hallway, she passed the sitting room and looked in. There was a huge bay window, you could see the sea, and a sailboat rested on a small table. Books on the shelves on either side of the fireplace and a round polished table with photos. Penny looked down the hallway and then went over to the table and looked down at the photos. A picture caught her eye, it was a photo of Ethan in a kilt and he was standing next to a woman whom she presumed was his late wife. She was beautiful, with auburn coloured hair and they both looked so happy.

"Are you lost?" said a voice, Penny quickly turned around. Mary stood with her arms folded and gave Penny a scowl.

"Sorry, I just wanted to" Penny held her towel even tighter.

"The kitchen is this way," said Mary curtly nodding to the hallway. Penny followed her out.

It was a huge kitchen, with an AGA set within a fireplace. A long table that could easily seat ten people and hanging from the ceiling was an old-fashioned drying rack for clothes.

"Give me your wet clothes," Mary said holding out her hand.

Mary made Penny feel extremely nervous and when Penny gave her the clothes, Penny let go of her towel and she felt it slip down to the floor. Penny was completely naked. At that point, Ethan had come into the kitchen, and Ellen was behind him. Penny was mortified and frantically tried to pick up the towel.

Penny could not turn around and look at Ethan, Ellen burst out laughing.

Penny frantically put the towel around her. Mary did not make eye contact with her and put the wet clothes on the table.

"Penny dear, follow me I will show you where you can get changed," said Ellen trying desperately not to laugh.

Penny closed her eyes and slowly turned around. She opened her eyes and Ethan was in his police uniform, he raised his eyebrows, and as she walked past him, he leaned in and whispered.

"I bet you wished you never got out of bed this morning," he had a wicked glint in his eyes. She looked at the floor and hurried out of the kitchen. Ellen was waiting for her in the hallway.

"Well, you certainly put a smile on Ethan's face again, never a dull moment with you Penny, there is a cloakroom in there," she pointed to the door, her eyes alight.

Penny smiled at her and quickly went in, she heard Ellen giggling to herself. Penny quickly dressed, cursing to herself. She took a deep breath and walked back into the kitchen.

Ethan was talking on his phone; Mary was by the AGA and Ellen was sitting down at the table.

"Come and sit down, do you want a coffee?" asked Ellen.

"There is none left," said Mary quickly, stirring a pot on the stove. Ellen pulled a face at Mary and got up and walked over to the kettle.

"Ellen it's fine honestly" Penny felt she needed to go now.

"Nonsense, lassie you have time for a coffee," said Ellen in a bossy tone.

Mary turned around and looked at Ellen and glared at her.

Ethan got off the phone and opened the cupboard in the corner of the kitchen.

"Are you working on your birthday, Ethan?" Penny hovered by a chair.

"Yep, not my choice, but hey it's overtime," he was fiddling with his belt.

"Happy Birthday, by the way," Penny said nervously.

He smiled in acknowledgement.

"So, I hear you are coming tonight," Ellen now came to sit down at the table.

Mary stormed out of the kitchen.

"Ethan what is her problem?" said Ellen crossly.

"How should I know?" Ethan was now fiddling with his uniform.

Penny slowly sat down at the table feeling uncomfortable. Ellen leaned into Penny.

"Mary was Mr Dalgleish...... Ethan's father in-law's housekeeper. Ethan and Susan kept her on when the old boy died," said Ellen giving her a nod.

Mary then returned to the kitchen and the atmosphere was even more frosty.

The kettle had boiled, and Ellen got up to make the coffee.

"So tonight, will be small, but it will be fun I am sure," said Ellen excitedly.

"I have work tomorrow remember, so it will be calm and civilised," Ethan was spinning his mobile phone around on the table one way and then spinning it the other way.

"You are a boring old fart; you only turn forty once," said

Ellen exasperated filling up the coffee pot. Ethan looked at Penny, then looked at his watch.

"Right, I have to go, Penny do you want a lift?"

"She hasn't had her coffee," Ellen said passing the coffee to Penny.

"Fine, I can wait ten minutes," Ethan sighed, sitting back in his chair.

Sammy came into the kitchen. He had a huge smile on his face, though it slightly dropped when he saw Penny.

"Sammy, I have to go to work, but aunt Ellen will look after you and then tonight you are staying with your friend Rory and his mum will take you to school tomorrow," Said Ethan with a big smile, Sammy came up to him and hugged him.

"Hello Sammy," Penny said smiling at him. Sammy shyly looked away and then ran out of the kitchen.

"That boy needs a mother," said Mary not looking at anyone.

"So tonight, the dress is smart casual, the rest of the family will be here for about seven, so come for then," Ellen glared at Mary.

"How many are coming?" Penny wished; she had never agreed to come.

"Oh, about twenty or so," said Ellen,

Ethan rolled his eyes and looked at his watch.

"Right let's go" Ethan stood up, putting his jumper on.

"Ethan, let her finish the coffee," protested Ellen

"No, it's fine I should be getting back," Penny got up.

"See you tonight Ellen....Mary," Penny gave them a nod.

"Won't be coming," said Mary gruffly stirring something on the AGA.

They walked out to Ethan's car. As Penny was putting her seat belt on, she turned to him.

"I must apologise about before, Ethan, I seem to be half-naked or naked around you, I am honestly not like this normally," Penny blushed in embarrassment.

"If you say so," He smiled with his eyes and drove off.

Ethan stopped on the verge outside the cottage. He turned to look at Penny.

"Penny, I know I kissed you last night and I am sorry if I stepped out of line. If you just want to be friends that is fine with me," he said quickly.

Penny leant over and kissed his cheek and pulled back.

"There is no need to be sorry, Ethan. I think we should just take one day at a time," before she could finish her sentence, he pulled her towards him and kissed her on her lips. Penny leant back from him stunned.

"What?" Ethan frowned.

"I just don't get you... one minute you seem annoyed with me the next you kiss me, I am just getting mixed messages," Penny leaned back in her seat and turned her head.

"Penny, I like you, a lot. I just find it hard to express my feelings. Also losing Susan has been hard". He looked out of the window.

"Ethan, I will see you tonight, and I think it would be best if we just take things incredibly slowly," she tapped his shoulder.

"Yes, you are right" he sighed.

"Look I finish my shift at six tonight, so I could come after and take you to the party?" He turned on the engine.

"That would be lovely, I will see you then," Penny gave him a peck on his cheek and got out of the car.

"Hang on I need your number. Just in case I am running late," he took his phone out of his trouser pocket.

"I don't have a phone," Penny quietly said.

"Why?" Ethan turned off the engine.

"I just felt I needed just to go off-grid for a while."

"Messy breakup?" Ethan sounded a little jealous.

"Something like that," Penny looked out to the sea.

"Well, if I am not here at six-thirty, you may have to make your own way," he gave a quick smile.

"That's fine," she gave him a wave and watched him drive off.

Penny gave a heavy sigh and kicked the ground with frustration.

"Why do I have to make things so complicated?" she squealed.

CHAPTER 6

Penny frantically got ready at about five that afternoon. She had no clothes, and nothing could pass for smart casual. Again, she was wearing the same old clothes, they must have thought she was very odd. Tomorrow, she had to find a clothes shop on the island if it was the last thing she did. It was almost coming up to six o'clock, Penny sat on the sofa nervously waiting for Ethan.

She heard a car pull up outside and Penny quickly stood up and looked out of the window. It was not Ethan. A man and woman got out of the car. They were both wearing suits and sunglasses. They looked like they were from the FBI. They walked up the path, Penny opened the front door.

"Can we come in Penny; we are from the police?" Said the man looking nervously over his shoulder and then edged forward and rested his foot on the threshold.

"Someone is coming here very soon, so you will need to be quick," Penny looked behind them.

"Penny, just checking in really," said the woman who had a weird little tattoo on her hand, she spoke with a harsh London accent.

"Yes, all good," Penny nodded her head.

"Well just to let you know that we have had word that Jason, Mr Hart has been formally charged and will now be awaiting trial, which I am sure you will be relieved about. So, we will be moving you back to London at the end of the week, as the Prosecution team will need to talk to you. You will still be under Witness Protection in a safe house. Alec will be informed what time on Friday," said the man, who seemed familiar to Penny.

"Right," Penny said, slightly overwhelmed by the news. She was going back to London, it happened so quickly. Penny thought she would be here for longer. At that point Ethan pulled up in his car and slowly got out, he was still wearing his police uniform.

"Right, we will go," said the man nervously and they quickly walked to their car and got in. Ethan looked at them for some time and then came up the path.

"Who were they?" said Ethan turning to look at them drive off.

"Not sure they needed directions" Penny felt overcome with emotion.

"Strange…" Ethan turned to look at the road, the car had now gone.

"Penny …everything ok?" Ethan cocked his head.

"Yes fine, let me get my things, won't be a minute."

Penny hurried inside and stood looking around the living room. She was leaving, Penny had to slow things down with Ethan, but her heart was ruling her head. This was such a mess. She was excited that she would be going home, though the idea of sitting in a courtroom and seeing Jason scared her. She felt as if she was going to have a panic attack.

"You can do this, "Penny said to herself.

She got her bag and coat and convinced herself, that Ethan would be understanding. She could always say a family emergency had come up and when the court case had finished, she would contact Ethan. It would be fine, she said over and over in her mind.

"Penny, we have to go," said Ethan impatiently

"Coming..." Penny came out and locked the door.

"Now my family is a little full-on, I have to warn you now," Ethan said quickly walking to the car. Penny got into the car and put her seat belt on and took a deep breath. Maybe she should tell Ethan the truth, after all, he is a policeman. He got in and threw his cap into the back seat and put on his seat belt and turned to look at Penny.

"Are you sure you are ok?" Ethan turned the engine on.

"Ethan, I may have to go back... to London on Friday, slight family problem," Penny said nervously.

"I see, and how did they contact you... smoke signals?" he said laughing.

"What... yes, no I mean I rang them earlier, from a phone box" Penny blurted out, quite pleased with her quick thinking.

"Nothing serious I hope?" he said pulling onto the road.

"No, long story," Penny let out a huge sigh of relief.

They pulled into the drive; it was full of cars.

"Oh, I really can't be doing with this, I just wanted a quiet night," He got out and slammed his car door.

Ethan walked up to the front door and it flew open. There was a rather large man, with white hair and a ruddy complexion, wearing a very bright waistcoat. He stood with a glass of whisky and he looked three sheets to the wind already.

"My boy," said the man in a very loud booming voice.

"Uncle James, I see you have pinched my whisky," said Ethan and took the glass and downed it, winced and handed it back to him.

"Uncle James, this is Penny... Penny this is my Uncle James," Ethan walked straight past him and left Penny standing at the door.

"Hello, Penny, lovely to meet you, come in.... come in" He held the door open and Penny walked in.

"I am Ellen's father; she has told me so much about you," He said following Penny up the hallway. Penny walked into the sitting room and there were certainly more than twenty people. More like fifty.

Ellen spied Penny from the other side of the room and bounded over.

"You're here," she said almost falling over. Penny put her hand out to steady her.

"Whoops I think my drinks have been a little too strong, must calm down," Ellen beamed a huge smile.

Penny looked around the room and standing by the fireplace, was a tall woman, about Penny's age. She was very striking, she had fire red hair and her eyes were almost violet. She was beautifully dressed; she certainly did not look like a local.

The woman walked over to Penny and Ellen.

"Ellen who is your friend?" said the woman in a strained voice, her eyes piercing.

"This is Penny... Penny this is Olivia. We were best friends at school and then she left me and went to Edinburgh and became a doctor," said Ellen sighing.

"Penny," said Olivia in a snotty tone and gave a smile.

Olivia turned to look at someone who had just come into the room, she then turned back and gave another smile to Penny.

Ethan came into the room; he was wearing a white shirt and a suit and looked extremely handsome. Penny felt weak. The idea of leaving him was unbearable. Olivia made a beeline straight for Ethan and flung open her arms. He looked shocked to see her and kissed her on her cheek.

"I didn't think she would come," said Ellen under her breath.

"Sorry," Penny looked down at Ellen, now desperate for a drink.

"She has become so high and bloody mighty. She broke Ethan's heart and now he is single she is back, the vulture. He better not, she is so false and ...." Ellen took a gulp of her drink.

"Sorry Penny where are my manners, would you like a drink?" Ellen now walking over to the drinks table. Penny followed her intrigued by Ethan and Olivia.

"So why did they break up?" Penny whispered to Ellen.

Ellen turned around and took Penny to one side.

"Well, we were all at school together and he loved her, I

mean big fat love fest for Olivia. He did everything for her, followed her around like a lovesick puppy. Eventually, she agreed to go out with him, they dated on and off and he was besotted with her. Now her mother, who you have met...."

Penny interrupted her, frowning.

"Have I?" Penny looked over at Olivia.

"Aye, Mary," Ellen said whispering.

Penny looked over at Olivia who was standing preening herself, and now and again touching Ethan's arm which made Penny incredibly jealous.

"Anyway, to cut a long story short, Mary did not want her precious Olivia, her only daughter to settle with a local, so she made sure they didn't get together. Olivia was never into Ethan anyway. Then a few years later, Ethan met Susan. She was young and impressionable only seventeen, and she became pregnant with Sammy a few years later and so Ethan did the honourable thing and married her. Well, her father made sure he did." She said now giving Penny a drink at long last.

"How did Susan die? Sorry, that was out of line?" Penny took a big gulp of her drink.

Ellen looked at her and was about to say when someone came over and started to chat with Ellen.

Penny looked over at Ethan and said to herself "you are going on Friday, just forget him." Ethan made his excuses with Olivia and came over to Penny.

"Are you having a good time?" Ethan looked around the room.

"Yes," Penny looked down at the floor.

Ellen came over and stood next to them. Then realised that she was a gooseberry and made an excuse and left.

"Ethan I am not feeling that well, I may just go," Penny placed her glass down on a side table. He was about to speak when Olivia came over.

"Penny, so how do you know Ethan?" Olivia stood with one hand on her hip and the other arm draped over his shoulder and pulling Ethan so tightly.

"Oh, you know," Penny picked up her glass and took a sip of her wine.

"No, I don't know," she said glaring at Penny, she suddenly gave a smile "Oh I just love your blouse, it's Dior?"

"Olivia leave Penny alone, what's with all the questions?" Ethan gently moved her arm from his shoulder.

"I am just making conversation, as you know when a new person comes to the island tongues wag and everyone wants to know your business," she gave a quick smile to Penny. Penny noticed on Olivia's wedding finger a ring.

"Are you here with your husband Olivia?" Penny gave a strained smile, looking directly at her.

"Nope..., but that ship has sailed sort of...." she said hiding her hand now and looking uncomfortable.

Olivia leant forward,"Are you a spinster.... I mean not married?" Olivia looked Penny up and down.

Ethan rolled his eyes, embarrassed by their behaviour.

"Ladies I am going to have to mingle," Ethan pointed to the room.

Olivia and Penny watched him walk to the other side of the room.

"Right, I should mingle too, so good to be back in the bosom of Ethan's family again, I so have missed them," she said sighing.

"Bet you have," Penny said under her breath.

"Sorry," Olivia squinted her eyes at Penny.

"Nothing," Penny turned around to look at some people coming into the sitting room. She couldn't stand next to Olivia any longer and moved away from her and went to speak to Ellen.

"Ellen I am not feeling that great, so I think I will just go."

Ellen's face dropped.

"If you must," sounding a little annoyed. "I will run you home, this party isn't exactly jumping, and I am sure they won't miss me."

"No Ellen you stay, I will call a cab," looking over at Ethan and then a feeling came over her and quickly said "Actually I will be fine Ellen," giving a smile, tapping the rim of her wine glass.

"Okeydokey..." Ellen leant back from, giving Penny a puzzled look.

By eleven o'clock, it was only Ellen and Penny, all the other guests had gone. Penny walked into the sitting room, Ethan was collecting glasses, and he turned to look at her.

Penny took some glasses from the mantlepiece.

"Penny no need, Mary can do it tomorrow," He carried on placing the glasses on a tray.

Ellen came in and sat down on the sofa and kicked off her

shoes.

"Well, that was the most boring party....I am so sorry Ethan," Ellen stretched upwards, and then lay on the sofa.

"Oh, I wouldn't say that," Ethan glanced at Penny, smiling to himself.

Penny picked up a few more glasses, she turned and Ellen was fast asleep.

Ethan wandered over and smiled down at Ellen.

"She could never handle her drink," he whispered and picked up a blanket and draped it over her.

"Penny, can I have a word?" asked Ethan quietly, he gestured towards the kitchen.

They walked in, and Ethan stood behind Penny. He was so close; she felt his breath on her neck. She did not dare turn around and closed her eyes. She moved the other side of the kitchen.

"Ethan I am going back on Friday, and I am not sure when I will be back, so ..." Penny placed the glasses by the sink.

He walked over to her.

"I don't care, Penny I will still be here. Just please promise you will come back?" He reached out his hand and gently pulled her towards him.

"Ethan don't, it's not fair on us both. My life in London is complicated and I just can't get involved with anyone now," Penny stood back from him and let go of his hand slowly.

"Penny what is really going on?" he said moving closer.

"Ethan, it's complicated and that's all I can say," now

wishing she had just a little more time on the island.

He leant back on the AGA and folded his arms.

"Penny, is there really a family drama?" He leant forward.

"Yes," Penny nodded her head.

"Right, I will run you home," Ethan sounded a little hurt.

Penny followed him out and they walked in silence to the car. The roar of the sea could be heard. Penny waited for Ethan to open the car. They got in and Ethan turned to Penny and whispered,

"I have something for you," he smiled and leaned in the back and picked up a box and placed it on her lap.

"What is it?" Penny looked up at him.

"Open it," he sat back in his seat.

"Surely I should be giving you a present," Penny looked at the box.

He smiled and gestured she opened it.

Penny opened the box. She looked at him, his eyes alight. There were a pair of yellow wellingtons. Penny gave a slight laugh, then tears welled up and she began to cry.

"I thought you liked your weird duck boots?" Ethan was confused.

"I love them, it's the nicest thing anyone has...." she burst out crying again.

"Penny?" Ethan rubbed his face with his hands and looked over to her.

"Ignore me," she said in between breaths and fanning herself with her hands.

He turned on the engine and gave her a strained look.

She smiled down at the boots and then started to cry. He shook his head and drove off. Penny in the past, expected expensive presents from her boyfriends. Jewellery, holidays, and handbags. Though this to Penny was the best present.

He parked up outside the cottage and turned off the engine. Penny gave him a peck on the cheek and got out of the car.

"Thank you again for the boots, you didn't need to."

"Can I see you tomorrow?" Ethan turned on the engine.

"Yes," Penny whispered.

She watched him drive off, feeling utterly distraught.

CHAPTER 7

Penny awoke to someone knocking at the front door. She looked at the clock it was nine. She sat up and rubbed her face, the sunlight was streaming through the window. Penny wandered to the window and peered out, Alec was at the front door.

Penny opened the door, Alec frowned at her.

"Can I come in?" he looked nervously over his shoulder.

"Yes, excuse the mess," Penny went to sit back down on the sofa. He slowly walked in and sat on the chair opposite her. He looked around the room and rubbed his chin with his hand and took a deep breath.

"Right, so your ferry will leave at ten o'clock on Friday, someone will come to collect you," he stared at Penny.

"Thank you, Alec, for everything, you have been a real rock. Do you want a coffee...actually I have no milk, I should go and get some" Penny mumbled to herself.

"Your car at Ethan's?" Alec squinted his eyes at Penny.

"No why?" Penny shook her head.

Alec pointed to outside. Penny stood up and went to the front door and opened it. The car was gone.

"What, it was here last night," Penny groaned.

"Oh," Alec frowned.

"I am going to have to report it stolen, oh this is all I need," Penny slammed the door. Alec jumped with fright.

"Alec, give me five minutes, then can you run me to the police station?" Penny went into the bathroom and stood by the mirror, taking her makeup off.

"Let's not be hasty, maybe someone borrowed it?" said Alec.

Penny popped her head out of the bathroom, "No, it's been stolen…"

"Probably bairns, it will turn up," he said slowly standing up.

"No Alec, this is just a nightmare," Penny came storming out of the bathroom and brushed her hair. She took her makeup bag from the table and sat down, and began to apply her makeup.

"Penny, think about it; you can't draw attention to yourself," said Alec in a slight panic.

"No Alec, I have to report it, I will walk into town if I have to," Penny forcefully put her makeup back in her bag and grabbed her wellingtons and put them on.

"Fine lassie, though you are making a big mistake. Come around to mine in about ten minutes. I must sort something out," he stared at the floor, rubbing his chin.

Penny waited ten minutes and walked over to Alec's. He was waiting by his car.

Alec for once drove slowly into town, he didn't go over thirty. Penny looked over to Alec.

"Alec are you alright?" Penny narrowed her eyes.

"Aye," Alec concentrated on the road.

"It's just you normally drive fast..." Penny gave a quick smile.

"Not today..." he said gruffly.

They arrived in the town; it was busy. A ferry had arrived, and passengers were disembarking.

"I will wait in the car," he said nervously.

Penny walked into the small police station, and behind the counter were Ethan and a young policeman. Ethan stopped talking when she came in and gave her a warm smile.

"Penny," he smiled with his eyes.

Penny flung her bag on the counter.

"Ethan, my car has been stolen," she sighed.

The young police officer became excited and stood up. He had the most unfortunate complexion; it was red and slightly flaky. Ethan placed his hand on the policeman's shoulder and slowly pushed him down.

"Alan I will deal with this," Ethan lifted the counter and held it open and beckoned Penny through.

 "Right, we better file a report," Ethan sighed.

Penny dragged her bag along the counter and walked through to the office and sat down opposite Ethan. He brought out a file and was trying to find a pen. Penny looked around the office. There was a picture of Sammy on Ethan's desk.

"You have a good view," Penny nodded at the window to the side of his desk. Ethan smiled and carried on looking for the pen.

Penny turned to look at Alan, who was biting his fingernails and looking thoroughly bored. The fax machine started to beep. Alan excitedly got up and went over and watched the piece of paper slowly coming out of the machine.

Alan looked at it and sighed and placed it on the table. Penny noticed it was a picture of a woman and she could make out *Missing Person* at the top of the page. Alan took some drawing pins from a small pot and picked up the piece of paper and forcefully stuck the pins in, he stood back from the noticeboard.

"So, we know the make, Fiat, do you know the registration, Penny?" asked Ethan. Penny looked up at Ethan, her eye was drawn to the Missing Person photograph, she leaned closer.

"Penny," Ethan waved his hand in front of her face.

"Hang on Ethan," Penny stood up and walked closer to the picture on the noticeboard.

"Penny I would really like to do this today," said Ethan annoyed, tapping the pen on the paper.

The photograph was of Penny. It was a photograph taken at her parent's house, last Christmas. Penny felt sick and confused, a coldness took over her body.

"Chief phone call for you," said another policeman from an office.

"Can it not wait John?" said Ethan now exasperated with the interruptions.

"No," said the policeman.

"Fine," Ethan threw the pen down and walked into the other office.

Penny stood looking at the photograph. Alan looked at Penny and then at the photograph.

"She looks a little like you, except she has blonde hair, and is a little chubbier," Alan said smiling.

"Yes…… I mean no," Penny snapped at Alan.

"Alan, can I ask you a question? "Penny picked up her bag, Alan nodded.

"Let us just say someone was under Witness Protection, would a missing person's report be filed?" Penny closed her eyes waiting for his response.

"Hmm… I guess not, why?" he sounded confused.

"Oh, it's for the article, I am writing…So no then…?" Penny's mind was racing.

"No, the unit wouldn't allow it. Even if the family reported it," Alan was fiddling with a rubber band.

"Alan it is really important, can you ……" Penny heard Ethan finishing his phone call.

"I have to go…" Penny rushed out of the police station. In a blind panic, Penny ran across the street. Alec was sitting in the car and did not see her. She saw Ellen opening the shop and quickly ran up behind her and pushed her in, the bell frantically ringing above them.

"Lock the door," Penny whispered out of breath.

"Penny, what has got into you?" Ellen frowning.

"Shh… let me think a moment," Penny frantically ran her hands through her hair, she was muttering to herself.

"Penny you are really scaring me," Ellen walked away from Penny.

"Ellen something has happened, I can't quite work out what is going on. I think I am in real danger, and I need your help," Penny grabbed Ellen's hands. There was a knock at the door, and someone tried the door handle, and the bell gave a little ring.

"Don't let them in," Penny whispered and pulled Ellen to the back of the shop. They waited for a while and the person seemed to have gone.

"Come in the back," Ellen pushed Penny around the counter.

"Penny, will you please tell me what's going on?" Ellen pleaded.

"Ellen, about two weeks , I was at my ex-boyfriend's house at a party."

Ellen nodded her head.

"His name is Jason and that night I found out that he was basically a gangster..."

Ellen gasped and covered her mouth.

"It gets worse, I witnessed...I witnessed" Penny couldn't get the words out.

"What did you witness?" Ellen's eyes darting around.

"Ellen, what do you know about Alec?" Penny frantically whispered.

"Why do you want to know about Alec?" Ellen looked confused.

"How long has Alec lived on the island?" Penny was chewing her thumbnail.

"Well, he came here about twenty-five years ago after his wife died ..." Ellen suddenly stopped herself and covered her mouth with her hands.

"Ellen, what is it?" Penny whispered.

"Alec came over with his grandson, who was called Jason," her lips trembling, she turned away from Penny.

"Jason's father was in prison; his mother had died; it was the talk of the island." Ellen tightly held her hands together, her eyes full of fear.

"How old was Jason when he arrived on the island?" Penny now pacing around.

"Let me see, he would have been around ten or twelve," Ellen stared at the floor.

"That would make sense, Jason is about thirty-seven," Penny looked over at the shop door.

"Penny I am confused, what have Alec and Jason got to do with you being here?"

"The police said I was under Witness Protection; I went to the police...they said it would be safer if I was away until there was a court case...they, whomever they are. Last night a man and woman came to the cottage and told me I am going back to London on Friday. Just now I was at the police station, a Missing Person photo came through, it's me," Penny took a deep breath.

"We have to tell Ethan." Ellen walked to the shop door.

"I need to escape and go back to London and tell the police, the real police, I witnessed the murder," Penny frantically whispered.

"Murder?" whispered Ellen, her eyes wide.

"Yes, Jason shot a man, I witnessed it at the party. The policeman I made the statement to must know Jason and tipped him off, it is the only explanation. Though it does not explain why they brought me up here, why not kill me?"

"Ellen, tell Alec that I have taken the bus to the next town to go clothes shopping and that he should go home. I will get the next ferry out of here and make my way back down to London," a rush of adrenalin took over Penny.

"He won't believe me, there is no other town on the island, and there is no other clothes shop." Ellen was holding her hands in agitation.

"Seriously there is no clothes shop?" Penny gave a surprised look.

"No, I order clothes for people and they pick them up..." Ellen said in a daze.

There was another knock at the door and the door handle was tried again. They both looked at each other.

"Ellen," said a voice, it was Alec. Again, he tried the door with more force this time.

Ellen pointed upstairs and they quietly walked to the back of the shop, and she ushered Penny to go upstairs.

"Go upstairs and hide in the bathroom. I will get rid of him," she whispered.

Penny crept up the stairs and walked into the small flat. It was cosy, the floors were stripped, and a wood burner in the fireplace, with a basket of logs next to it. On the walls were paintings, mostly of the sea. A cream sofa by the window, with a light blue tartan rug, draped over the arm.

Penny hurried into the bathroom and closed the door and locked it, she heard the bell above the door ring and there were muffled voices from downstairs. After five minutes, the bell went, and Penny slowly moved over to the window in the bathroom. She peered out and saw Alec walking slowly to his car. He got in and drove off.

Penny let out a sigh of relief and crept down the stairs.

"Can I come out now?" Penny whispered.

"All clear," Ellen beckoned her over.

The shop door opened, and they both jumped, Ethan stormed in.

"You scared me," Ellen clutched her chest, taking deep breaths.

"You called me, what's going on you sounded in a panic?" he said with a worried look on his face.

"Why did you do that?" Penny angrily whispered to Ellen.

"I didn't have a choice, Penny; this is bloody serious," Ellen whispered angrily.

"Will someone please tell me what is going on?" Ethan marched up to them.

Ellen raced over to the shop door and locked it and pushed Ethan to the back of the shop.

"Penny," Ellen nodded at her.

"Right fine…" Penny snapped, clutching her head in her hands.

"Ethan, how much do you know about the Witness Protection Unit?" Penny whispered.

"Not much why?" He took his cap off and wiped his forehead with his arm.

"Two weeks ago, I was at my ex-boyfriend's party…"

Ethan interrupted her.

"I haven't got time for any ex-boyfriend dramas, is this why you called me over?" He said exasperated with Ellen.

"Ethan will you just shut up and let Penny finish," Ellen hit his arm.

"Well at the party…" Ethan interrupted again.

"Yes, we got that part, at the party" He was now trying to speed Penny up, with a gesture of his hands and then looking at his watch.

"Am I keeping you?" Penny asked, folding her arms.

"As a matter of fact, yes you are, I have to be back at the police station, and you need to fill out that report," Ethan rested his hands on his hips, glaring at Penny.

"Ethan, will you stop interrupting her," Ellen hissed.

"I witnessed my ex shooting a man in the head," Penny looked at Ethan, all the colour now draining from his face.

"Is this some joke?" Ethan was stunned; Penny shook her head.

"What happened after you saw the shooting?" Ethan folded his arms.

"I went to the police in London and then they said they were going to put me under Witness Protection and ended up here."

"How do you know you are not under Witness Protection?" Ethan looked even more confused.

"The fax of the missing woman, that came through this morning is me," Penny said thumping her chest.

"Ethan, what do we do?" Ellen clutched her hands.

" I need to think," he said waving his hand at Ellen.

"Does anyone else know? Ethan whispered; Ellen looked at Penny.

"Penny, Ellen who else knows?" he became agitated and looked at his watch.

"Alec," Penny whispered.

"Alec, why the hell is he involved?" Ethan exclaimed.

"Ethan, do you remember Jason his grandson?" said Ellen quietly.

"Sort of, he was a few years below me at school, why?" Ethan stood tapping his cap on his leg.

"Jason, is my ex," Penny whispered.

"Who brought you here Penny, if that is your real name?" Ethan moved closer to Penny.

"Penny is my real name, they just changed my surname, they gave me the surname Hargreaves, my surname is Brown. A policeman drove me here, well I thought he was a policeman," Penny hugged herself.

"I am going back to the station and will find out what is going on. I will investigate your missing person report. Penny, stay here above the shop. Do not move until I come back. Ellen, keep the shop open, though if anyone comes in who is not a local just call me."

Ethan walked to the door, he stopped and turned.

"Penny, the man, and woman who came yesterday, who were they?" he said calmly.

"I don't know Ethan, it's all such a mess, please help,"

Penny said desperately.

"Leave it to me, though please just don't go AWOL, stay on the island, it may not seem like it but is the safest place for you now."

"You have to trust me Penny."

CHAPTER 8

Penny went upstairs and waited in Ellen's sitting room. Ellen stayed downstairs and now and again would check on Penny. She heard the door of the shop go a few times and each time Penny jumped with fear.

Penny heard footsteps coming up the stairs, she got up from the sofa and waited for the person to come in. The door opened and Ellen briskly walked in.

"Right, would you like tea?" Ellen went into the kitchen and flicked the switch.

"No, I am all right.." Penny sat down on the sofa.

"You have a lovely place Ellen," Penny called to her.

Ellen popped her head around the door "Thank you," she gave a warm smile.

"I love the paintings, where did you buy them?" Penny stood up and looked at them.

"I didn't.." Ellen came out, she was holding her hands tightly.

"Oh, ..." Penny looked back at the paintings.

"I mean, I painted them…" Ellen gave a quick smile.

"They are amazing Ellen; you have a real talent," Penny exclaimed.

"I tried to sell them, though no one wanted them…" Ellen

gave a heavy sigh.

"I am surprised...Well, these would go for a lot of money in London. I know someone who owns a gallery, they would snap them up," Penny said excitedly.

"Really...?" Ellen frowned.

"Yes, I will contact them, if and when I get back down to London," Penny raised her eyebrows.

"You will...Ethan will sort it out...right I will go back down and will pop up later."

An hour later, Ethan returned, he walked into the sitting room, looking concerned.

"Penny, sit down," Ethan said quietly.

"I am going to have to be quick, as I must get back to the station. The report was filed by your parents a week ago. Apparently, they came to visit you, the night you were taken. The next day they came back and bumped into your neighbour, who told them she had seen you getting into a car with your suitcase. The neighbour said you looked slightly upset. When they could not get hold of you on your mobile, they rang your work, who said you had not been in and you had not requested leave.

Ethan took a deep breath.

"Jason has been seen in Glasgow; a couple of days ago, he is known to the police there. It makes sense, as he moved back there when he was fifteen, when his father was released from prison. I checked the deeds of The Lookout and he is the owner," Ethan took Penny's hands in his.

"Penny, you have to be honest with me and don't bite off my head, though have you ever been involved in Jason's

"......" Penny interrupted Ethan.

"Ethan, you must believe me, I never knew about what Jason did. I only found out the night of the party.... But....." Penny bit her bottom lip.

"Penny..." Ethan came close to her, his eyes darting around her face.

"I may have taken a teeny-weeny object from his house the night of the party," she closed her eyes and clenched her fists.

"And what was this teeny-weeny thing, Penny?" Ethan said through gritted teeth.

"Alright, the night of the party, he was flirting all night with this girl. I knew he was probably sleeping with her..."

"Penny just get to the point.." Ethan snapped.

"When I was in the bathroom, I knocked over some toiletries, when they fell to the floor, a can of hairspray..."

Ethan cocked his head and gestured with his hand for her to hurry.

"It had a false bottom and these lovely pair of diamond earrings fell out," Penny looked at the floor.

"So, you stole from a psychopath...just great..." Ethan turned from her and clasped his head in his hands.

"So they kept you alive because you have the earrings.." Jason glared at Penny.

"Yes probably..." Penny hugged herself and slowly sat down on the sofa.

"Penny, Jason is not some small-time gangster. He has links with some pretty dangerous people."

Ellen barged into the room, she was out of breath and clutching her chest.

"Ethan, two guys have been in, they are not locals, have Glaswegian accents and look mean," she said out of breath.

"Ellen, are you sure you haven't seen them before?" Ethan looked out the window. Ellen came up behind him and peered out the window.

"Those two over there," she said excitedly, pointing at the men.

"Ellen, do you want to shout that any louder," he said pulling her away from the window. Penny looked out the window and saw the men standing across the road. Penny let out a gasp.

"What?" Ethan exclaimed.

"The younger one, he was the policeman who took my details at the police station in London," Penny backed away from the window.

"You are not safe here. It will take a day for any support from the mainland to come over." Ethan rubbed the back of his neck.

"Ethan what about Moray?" Ellen slowly sat down.

"No, it's too dangerous," Ethan shook his head.

"It makes sense, no one knows about the island and also it might give you time to call in back up," said Ellen her eyes alight.

"Ellen, you watch too many police dramas," Ethan scoffed.

"Can someone explain to me about Moray," Penny now

slightly exasperated by the two of them bickering.

"Moray is a small island to the west of here. During the Second World war, they built some lookouts, they are more like cottages. They were built in case Germans came here. I check on the island now and again, MOD thing," Ethan sighed.

"Ethan surely with your training, you could get Penny there, lie low and wait for the cavalry," Ellen said excitedly.

"Training what training?" Penny said a little flustered.

"You haven't told her?" Ellen raised her eyebrows.

"No, I haven't told her Ellen," Ethan rubbed his face.

Penny looked at Ethan waiting for him to explain.

"Ok when I was eighteen, I joined the Navy and then briefly… very briefly I was in the SBS. I hated it by the way," flopping down into a chair.

The bell went, and they all looked at each other.

"Ellen did you not lock it?" Ethan glared at Ellen "Go down now Ellen and whomever it is tell them you are closing early for stocktaking," Ellen nodded her head and quickly went downstairs.

A few seconds later the shop bell rang, and Ethan peered out the window.

" It's a local," Ethan sighed.

Ellen came up the stairs again out of breath.

"Ok, we will go to Moray after my shift tonight. We will wait until dark; Ellen I need Uncle James's boat; can you just tell him to moor it over at mine, in the bay." Ethan looked at his phone.

"What shall I tell him, won't he think it odd?" Ellen pulled a face.

"Tell him there is a bottle of whisky in it for him and not to ask any questions," Ethan exasperated with Ellen.

"Ok, but you can't leave Penny on her own on the island," Ellen hissed.

"She won't be on her own, I will stay with her. I have luckily two days off, starting from tomorrow. I will call the mainland when I am out there, hopefully, by the morning there will be back up, as you call it," Ethan raised his eyebrows at Ellen.

Ethan walked to the door and rested his hand on the handle.

"Penny quick question..." he turned to look at her.

"Yes..." Penny took a step closer to him.

"You can swim, can't you?" He cocked his head.

"Yes...why?" Penny frowned at Ethan.

"Just needed to know.." and he quickly left.

"Wow, this is all so surreal," Penny sat down not quite believing what was happening.

"Oh, you poor thing, let me make you a sweet tea and we can get a bag together for you. Penny, you have certainly livened things up here. I know this is not your choice, though since you have come to the island... I don't know it's like you were meant to come into our lives." Ellen walked into the small kitchen across from the sitting room. Penny followed her in and stood in the doorway.

"Thank you, Ellen," Penny burst into tears.

"Hey, no tears, you need to focus on tonight. Ethan will

protect you," Ellen smiled at Penny.

"I am so sorry you have both got caught up in this mess, it's all my fault. If I hadn't been so greedy and taken those earrings..." Penny wiped the tears from her eyes.

"I am sure tomorrow; it will have all been sorted. I will get you those clothes. You will need some proper shoes, not those boots" she said turning to the cupboard and then there was an almighty crash from downstairs, they both jumped.

Ellen leaned over Penny and opened the kitchen door slightly and behind it, she brought out a baseball bat, Penny flinched.

"You can never be too careful," Ellen whispered.

Ellen slowly went down the stairs, Penny followed her and then she stopped suddenly. They moved down a few more steps. A figure came out of the shadows, they both screamed. Ellen lifted the baseball bat.

"It's me, Jimmy," he said panicked and raising his arms to protect himself.

"Jimmy MacDonald, what are you doing sneaking around?" Ellen whispered angrily putting the baseball bat down.

"I saw the back door of the shop was open and thought I would check it out. I knocked over all your paraphernalia down the corridor there...hang on you were going to hit me?" Jimmy now leaning back from them.

"Well, if the shop is closed and we hear a crash, we are going to come down prepared," Ellen huffed.

"Why is the shop closed?" Jimmy hissed.

"Excuse me, this is my shop, is not yours anymore. If you hadn't been cavorting with tarty Jean, you would have a say," Ellen repeatedly thumped the baseball bat on the floor.

Penny slowly walked back up the stairs and left them arguing. Penny went into the sitting room and walked over to the window and looked out. A few cars drove down the road, people getting on with their daily lives, though Penny felt her life had stopped. She was deep in thought and did not hear Ellen come into the room.

"I am so sorry Penny, this is the last thing you need," Ellen rested the baseball bat up against the wall.

"To be honest, it takes my mind off things…sorry that came out wrong," Penny held her hand up.

"No need to apologise, I know what you mean. Well, we are a right pair. Men who needs them," said Ellen going back into the kitchen.

"Well of course excluding Ethan, he is one of the good ones," Ellen called from the kitchen. Penny smiled to herself, yes Ethan was one of the good ones.

"Tea will be ready soon; do you want anything to eat?" Ellen was clattering around in the kitchen. Penny walked over to Ellen.

"Ellen if for any reason I don't get back to London, can you contact my parents and tell them I am sorry," Penny began to cry.

"Hey Ethan, won't let anything happen to you. He is a mean lean fighting machine," she said laughing and hugged Penny. A text then came through on Ellen's phone. She took her phone out of her pocket.

"It's Ethan, change of plan, you are leaving now. He wants to go there in daylight as apparently there is a storm coming in," she said with a worried look on her face. Ellen phoned her father and convinced him to let Ethan use the boat.

"Right, you will need a hat a warm jacket, and some shoes," Ellen went into her bedroom and got the clothes and stuffed them into a bag.

"Ethan is going to meet us around the back, he wants you to travel in the boot if that's ok?" said Ellen out of breath.

Penny nodded and they quickly went down the stairs to the back door of the shop. They waited there for a couple of minutes and there was a knock at the door.

"Now," whispered Ethan and Ellen opened the door, his car was parked directly outside, the engine running. He beckoned Penny over and Ellen gave her a hug and whispered "You take care and once this is over, you and I are going for a very large drink."

Ethan opened the boot and Penny got in, the boot closed, and it was pitch dark.

CHAPTER 9

Ethan drove fast, Penny was thrown from side to side. A car-jack kept rolling into her head every time they went around a corner.

Penny felt the car slowing down, it stopped with a jolt. Ethan got out of the car and she heard Ethan walking around to the boot.

"Everything ok in there?" Ethan whispered.

"Would you be?" Penny shouted.

"Penny you will have to stay in there for a little longer, I need to change out of my uniform and get a few things," he said and tapped the boot.

"Ethan, you cannot leave me in here any longer," Penny kicked the boot

"Hey, keep it down, don't tell me you suffer from claustrophobia as well as vertigo?" he hissed.

"Ethan…" Penny protested and again kicked the boot.

"Will you just calm down and I will be five minutes, I promise, just keep quiet," He whispered. Penny heard him walking away from the car, his feet crunching along the gravel.

The jumper Ellen had given her was woollen and itched, it was getting too hot. There was a hole at the side of the boot. She tried to turn herself around and strained her neck to reach the hole. Cool air was slowly drifting in. She could hear some seagulls and the wind now and again blew over the car, the car rocking.

Eventually, she heard footsteps walking along the gravel.

"Ethan is that you?" Penny whispered.

"Yes, let's get you out, I need you to follow me quickly to the gate, where you came in the other day. You will have to keep close to me. Once we get to the bottom, get into the RIB and we will travel down the coast. Uncle James could not moor his boat here. We will transfer there onto his boat," he said quickly.

"RIB?" Penny whispered.

"Penny please stop asking questions, Mary is in the house, and she may think it odd seeing me talking to the boot of my car," he said whispering.

"Just get me out," Penny shouted.

He put the key in and opened the boot, the light flooding in. Penny covered her eyes from the brightness.

A car came down the gravel drive. Ethan pushed Penny down and closed it.

"Hey..." Penny shouted.

"Will you be quiet?" said Ethan said through gritted teeth.

It went silent and Penny heard the car stop, then a car door open and then close.

"Olivia," said Ethan surprised. Penny rolled her eyes and leaned against the boot trying to hear them.

"Ethan," said Olivia in a seductive tone.

"I just came to say goodbye before going back to Edinburgh,"

"Sorry Olivia, you have caught me at a bad time, I have to go back to the police station." He said nervously.

"Well, maybe we could do dinner after you have finished. I am staying at that cute little B&B, by the quayside?" Again, it fell silent, Penny was beginning to get hot again.

"Oh, I am not sure what time I will finish," he said quickly, and Penny could hear him shuffling around.

"Sorry, it's just I have missed you," she said quietly.

"Missed me?" Ethan stuttered.

"Are you really working or are you trying to fob me off?" Olivia sighed.

"No, I am working…." he tapped the car.

"Oh, I thought you might be seeing that sparrow Penny," Olivia said jangling her keys and leaning against Ethan's car.

Penny thumped the boot.

"Ethan your car has just made a noise," exclaimed Olivia.

"It does that sometimes, look I need to get going, how about I call you sometime?"

"Ethan everything ok, you seem jumpy?" she said concerned.

"Fine, long day," he sighed.

Penny tried to move to the hole, she could just make out Ethan's waist by Olivia's car. Penny moved closer and watched as Olivia moved in close to Ethan. Olivia traced her finger along his waist and said, "My room is 34, come by later..... and Ethan...." she said seductively, Ethan was trying to pull away.

"Yes," he sounded irritated and didn't look at Olivia.

"Don't change out of your uniform" she moved away from him and got into her car and drove off.

Ethan quickly walked back to the car, he opened the boot and Penny took a huge breath of air.

"Right go now," he said.

Penny ran down the path, the waves crashing down below. Ethan came up behind her and flicked the latch of the gate and pushed her through. Penny ran down the steps, feeling giddy at the sheer drop below.

"Come on slow coach," said Ethan trying to make Penny move faster.

The RIB was moored to the side of the jetty. Ethan threw the bag in the boat and held Penny's hand and Penny jumped in, almost falling over the side in the process.

Ethan quickly untied the rope and jumped in the boat. He started the motor and gestured with his hand she lay down. He sat at the back and flipped down his sunglasses and revved the motor more. They bounced through the waves, the boat jolting every time it went over a wave, the seawater swishing around their feet. Once they got further out to sea, Ethan cut the engine.

"We are going to drift for a little while," he said quickly turning to look at the beach. Penny nodded and held onto the rope at the side of the boat, she was starting to feel seasick.

"Uncle James' boat is moored, in a bay a few miles from here. It might be a little bumpy getting onto the boat," he said giving a slight sniff, taking off his sunglasses and wiping his forehead with his arm.

He was constantly looking around; the boat was bobbing up and down. Penny was feeling sick and leant over the boat and stared at the sea below.

"You, ok?" said Ethan now unzipping the bag and pulling out two dry suits and flippers.

Penny stared down at them, feeling dizzy.

"Right strip down to your knickers," he said taking out two face masks.

"What?" Penny exclaimed.

"You can swim, can't you?" he said now preoccupied with one of the dry suits and unzipped the back of it.

"Yes, but why can't we sail up to Uncle James' boat and climb aboard?" Penny was trying to steady herself.

"Penny, I don't have time for this, just undress and put your clothes and shoes in the bag," Ethan leaned forward and handed Penny the drysuit. She grabbed it from him and stood up,

"What are you doing?" he said holding on to the side of the boat.

"Getting into the wet suit," Penny looked down at him.

"Sit down, you will fall overboard and it's a dry suit," he said impatiently.

Penny sat down and started to undo her trousers and hesitated before pulling them down. He leant over, the spray of the sea going over the boat.

"I have seen it all before," he whispered and sat back and gave her a cheeky grin.

She looked away and tried to pull them off and because they were slightly wet, they got stuck around her ankles. Penny was yanking them, though they just wouldn't go over her feet.

"Really, you make such a drama out of everything," said Ethan his eyes glaring, and he knelt by her feet and grabbed her trousers and pulled them off. As he did so, a huge wave hit the side of the boat and Ethan fell on top of her. He pushed himself upwards and looked down at her.

"What?" Penny said the water swishing around her head, her hair soaking wet, the taste of sea salt making her feel queasy.

"Nothing," he said and quickly composed himself and sat back and ran his hands through his wet hair.

He took off his jumper and kicked off his trainers and took off his t-shirt. He was more athletically built than Penny thought. Not bulging muscles, but well-toned arms and he had a six-pack.

He looked at Penny "Can you hurry up; it will be dark in a few hours."

He handed her the dry suit and Penny quickly put it on, up to her waist. She took off her jumper and hesitated, before taking off her t-shirt.

"And your t-shirt…" Ethan sighed, he was taking off his jeans, and Penny found herself gazing at Ethan. Penny was not sure if it was the situation, though the feelings she had for Ethan were becoming so overwhelming. She had never been in love with someone. That deep-rooted love that you just cannot put into words. She was brought back down to earth when Ethan snapped, "Today Penny would be lovely."

He put the clothes in the bag. Penny quickly took off her t-shirt, the sun was beginning to set. She felt the coldness of the sea breeze, she had trouble trying to zip up the back.

Ethan leant forward and helped zip up her suit.

"Here are the flippers, they should fit you and a face mask," he was fiddling now with the rope on the boat and threw an anchor in.

"Do I have to fall back into the sea?" Penny nervously asked, looking around.

"Only if you want too?" he said collecting the rest of the clothes and putting them into the bag.

Penny put the flippers and facemask on and then sat on the side of the boat with her back to the sea and fell backwards. The sheer coldness of the water made her scream.

"It's freezing," she was bobbing up and down her teeth chattering.

Ethan placed the bag at the side of the boat and put his flippers and mask on and stood up and jumped in. He surfaced and put his arm over the side and picked up the bag and held it in the air and swam over to Penny.

"How come you get to jump in?" Penny taking in too much water and spluttering.

"I gave you the choice," he said now swimming away from her. Penny swam after him the waves were quite high and she had difficulty swimming through them.

"Around the corner is the boat, are you going to be, ok?" said Ethan shouting and treading water.

"Yes," she sighed and took in some water and started to

cough, her face stinging from the sea salt.

"Probably best if you keep your head up and don't speak. I don't want you drowning."

Ethan was a fast swimmer and Penny was struggling to keep up with him.

"Come on Penny, you are doing well, just focus on the cliff over there," he shouted.

Penny raised her hand in the air and was starting to feel tired. He swam back to Penny.

"Penny, I know this is hard, but you have to keep going, you can rest when you get to the island," he was trying not to laugh.

"What now?" Penny desperately trying to tread water.

"You look like a seal," he said smiling and then swam off.

"Duck, Seal… what next?" Penny said under her breath and swam after him.

They eventually came around the corner, the boat in the distance. It looked like a death trap. It was covered in rust it did not look seaworthy. Ethan got to the boat first. At the back of the boat, there was a ladder winched up.

"Keep the bag above your head," Ethan passed the bag to Penny.

With all her strength, she held it up above the waves. Ethan swam below the ladder and waited for a wave, the wave pushed him up and he caught the first run of the ladder and managed to pull it down. It made a very loud cranking noise and he swam back quickly to Penny and took the bag. Penny swam to the ladder and tried to grab it, though the waves were becoming stronger, and the strong current was pulling her away from the boat.

Ethan swam behind her and pulled her towards the ladder and directed her under it. She was trying to grab the ladder and kicked the bag from his hand. Penny watched as it drifted off and was caught up in a wave and crashed against a rock and then sank.

"Good one, no clothes are you a nudist or something?" he yelled at her.

"Do not blame me...it was an accident! Funnily enough, I can't control waves I am not God," Penny shouted and splashed him.

"Just get up there," he pushed her up to the ladder.

Penny grabbed the ladder and climbed up with her flippers on.

"Come on ducky get up there," Penny stopped and looked down at him and stuck her tongue out at him, he gave a little laugh and shook his head.

Penny eventually got to the top of the ladder and hauled herself over and collapsed on the deck. Ethan came up and pulled his flippers off and walked to the front of the boat.

Penny slowly pulled off her flippers and threw her face mask to the side. The boat was rolling from side to side.

Ethan ran his fingers at the top of the door leading into the cabin. He found a key and opened the door. Penny followed Ethan in, it was small and smelt of old fish and diesel.

Ethan started the engine, they crashed through the waves. Penny held onto a bar in front of her, the boat rising up and down.

Every time they hit a wave; Penny felt as if her neck was going to break.

"How far is the island?" Penny shouted.

"About an hour away," Ethan looked directly ahead.

"Really that long?" Penny shouted over the noise of the engine.

"Yes, look down below, there may be some blankets if you are cold."

It was now dark, and it began to rain. The waves were crashing over the front of the boat, it was freezing.

Penny went down the steps to the cabin below and sliding back and forth, were a couple of grey blankets. Penny grabbed them and went back up and handed Ethan a blanket and he shook his head. Penny wrapped it around her, and they jolted around, the waves now even higher.

"Right, we are about ten minutes away," Ethan turned to Penny and slowed the boat down.

"I thought you said it was an hour away," Penny almost fell backwards.

He gave a smile and raised his eyebrows. Penny pushed him and he stumbled backwards out of the cabin.

"Serves you right," Penny grabbed the steering wheel from him and took over and smiled at him.

"Impressed," said Ethan steading himself.

"My father has had boats all his life, we were forced every holiday on his boat, I hate them," Penny shouted.

"I am going to radio the Coast Guards and get them to contact the mainland, hopefully, they will meet us tomorrow at the quayside and we can take it from there."

Ethan took the receiver down and flicked the switch. It made a crackling noise, they heard a voice.

Ethan spoke to the Coast Guard and explained who he was and the situation. He was just about to give his coordinates when the radio cut out. Ethan hit the side of the radio, and nothing happened. He hit it again and it still was not working.

"Bloody fantastic," Ethan threw the receiver against the wall. Penny flinched.

"What about your phone?" Penny navigating the boat through a huge wave.

"Thanks to you it is at the bottom of the sea," he turned away from Penny and switched off the engine. It made a ticking noise, the sea spraying over the sides of the boat.

"We can't go back it is too risky and we don't have enough fuel to get to another island. We will have to stay on the island tonight and hope in the morning I have come up with a plan,"

"Could we not flag down another boat?" Penny pulled the blanket around her more.

"Because there are hundreds of boats floating by..." Ethan was trying to steady himself as a wave crashed over the boat.

"Let's go to the island and we can think of something," Penny turned on the engine and pushed the lever and they moved on.

CHAPTER 10

Penny glanced at Ethan; he was deep in thought.

"Ethan, I am sorry about the bag," Penny shouted.

"Don't worry, look I need to take over, there are too many rocks," he moved Penny out of the way. He slowed down the boat and flicked the switch above him and a light came on. Penny could just make out the island. The cliffs were high, and the clouds quickly moved across the moon. Ethan slowly guided the boat to a jetty at the side of the rocks. It was eerie, a coastal mist was coming in.

"Can you take the wheel?" he moved Penny in front of him.

Ethan ran to the front of the boat and quickly pulled the rope from inside the boat and swung it around the metal pillar on the jetty and pulled it tight.

"Cut the engine," he shouted.

Penny turned off the engine and there was silence again.

"Can you grab the blankets, there should be a jerrycan under the steering wheel." Ethan came in and went down below and then came up with a couple of bottles of water.

"I want you to go up first, use the ladder, it is quite old, so be careful. Are your feet going to be ok? The rocks are going to be quite sharp climbing up to the top there," Ethan moved the bottles of water outside the cabin.

"Ethan, I really can't thank you enough,"

"Well call it a busman's holiday," he was trying to sound positive, though Penny got the distinct impression he was now becoming genuinely concerned with the situation.

Penny slowly made her way up the ladder. It was rusty and wet, and she slipped a couple of times. Eventually, she got to the top and stood looking down at Ethan. He had found an old rucksack and put the water and a torch and blankets in and then swung it behind his shoulders and climbed up.

"Dam I forgot the jerrycan, wait here," he said handing Penny the rucksack.

He climbed down again and went into the cabin and came out with it.

"Stand back," he yelled, and Penny quickly moved backwards, and he threw it up to where she was and then climbed up.

"Right follow me and hold my hand."

He switched the torch on and grabbed her hand and Penny followed him up a path. They turned a corner, on a hill dug into it, were corrugated iron sheds and further up the path, was a small stone building. It was made of concrete and the front door was made of metal; he turned the handle. It would not open.

"What?" he exclaimed and tried the handle again.

"This shouldn't be locked," he said frustrated.

Ethan went to the side and lifted the window. It slowly opened, the rain started again, and the wind was blowing across the cliffs.

"Do you think you can get through Penny?"

"I can try."

Penny squeezed herself through the gap.

"The door should open from the inside," Ethan went to the front door and waited.

Penny stood looking around the room. There was a fireplace, an old wooden chair, and some wooden boxes.

"Penny, "Ethan shouted.

"Keep your hair on," she shouted back.

Penny yanked at the door and it slowly opened. Ethan came in with the rucksack and jerrycan and walked over to the chair and threw it against the wall.

Penny flinched.

"Feeling all right Ethan?"

He turned to look at her "We need fire wood."

He quickly gathered up the broken wood and threw it into the fire. He leant over and broke up the wooden boxes and put them to the side of the fireplace.

Penny walked to the window and looked out to the sea. The wind was howling and blowing through every crevice in the building. Ethan opened the bag and took out some matches and threw the contents of the jerrycan over the wood.

"Stand back," he lit a match and threw it at the wood. It did not do anything.

"Strange," he said scratching his head and lit another match and threw it and then there was an explosion of fire, smoke billowed from of the fireplace.

"Right take off your dry suit," He quickly took off his and laid it on the ground, next to the fire and got the blankets out of the rucksack.

Penny slowly took off her suit and he handed her a blanket.

"Not the most comfortable place, though it will do for tonight," he said wrapping the blanket around him and holding his hands out to the fire.

Penny slowly sat down next to Ethan and hung her head and started to cry.

"Hey, no tears on my watch. I know this is not your ideal situation. But it could be worse," he put his arm around her shoulders, giving her a squeeze.

Penny looked at him "How possibly could it be any worse?" bringing her knees up to her chest.

"Well, you could lose both your parents in a car crash at ten and then be put in care. Until your mad uncle and aunt take pity on you. And then at the age of eighteen, you find out the parents you mourned for were not your parents and you were adopted," Ethan stared at the fire.

Penny looked at Ethan.

"This happened to you?" Penny whispered.

Ethan nodded his head.

"So, Uncle James took you in?" Penny moved closer to Ethan.

"Yep, they were estranged from my adoptive parents. I grew up in Canada for the first ten years of my life. Uncle James' brother was my adoptive father. Apparently, they fell out over the family business and my adoptive father moved to Canada." Ethan looked down at the floor.

"Wow..." Penny gazed at him.

"Anyway, enough about me, what about you?" He held his hands out to the fire.

"Oh, I am boring," Penny sighed and picked up a piece of wood and tapped it on the ground.

"I don't think so; you have half of the London underworld after you..." Ethan gave Penny a nudge.

"What are we going to do?" Penny moved closer to the fire. Ethan was silent and then he stood up and walked to the window.

"Your idea about flagging down a boat might not be such a bad idea. Tomorrow when it gets light, we will look for a boat and use their radio," He said rubbing his hands to keep warm.

Penny nodded and stretched out; the room was feeling warm at last.

"Shall we take it in turns to get some shut-eye?" Penny lay back and looked at the ceiling.

"You want to sleep when we are having so much fun?" Ethan giggled.

He lay down and turned on his side, so he was facing Penny and stretched his hand out, so it was almost touching Penny.

"Yes, shut-eye might be a good idea, very welcome to use my chest as a pillow," he said tapping it.

"Ok then," Penny got up and moved towards him and lay down and rested her head on his chest.

"I didn't think you would," he mumbled and rested his

hand on her head.

Penny looked up at him "You look terrified," laughing.

He whispered, "I am," and he moved Penny off him and he sat back a little.

"Penny," he rubbed his face with his hands.

"Do you like me?" he brought his knees up to his chest.

Penny was taken aback and didn't answer.

"Ethan, why are you asking me this?" She leant forward.

"Sorry, it's just since Susan's death I have not been involved with anyone, not even a kiss. I have been trying to bring up Sammy or working. I am incredibly insecure and ……"

Penny got up and moved closer to him, she knelt in front of him and took his hands in hers.

"Yes," she whispered.

He pulled away and rubbed his face.

Penny lay back on the cold concrete floor and he leaned over her.

"Be gentle with me?" he said laughing and gently tucked her hair behind her ear.

"Shhh stop talking…." Penny whispered, kissing his lips.

CHAPTER 11

Penny awoke and looked at Ethan asleep next to her, the blankets wrapped around them. The fire was dying out and it was quite difficult to see in the room. Penny slowly moved away from Ethan and sat up, he stirred and turned onto his side.

Penny lay back down and could hear the waves crashing against the rocks. Then she heard what sounded like an engine. Penny strained to hear it, and quickly stood up and went to the window. She could just make out the jetty and saw their boat speeding across the waves. Penny ran over to Ethan and shook him.

"Ethan someone has taken the boat," she whispered.

He didn't wake up, "Ethan" she shouted.

"What?" he said startled and sat upright.

"Someone has taken the boat," Penny said in a panic.

"Are you sure?" he said dazed, rubbing his face.

"Yes," Penny picked up her dry suit and quickly put it on.

Ethan got a bottle of water and threw it on the fire.

"We need to go," trying to put on his drysuit.

"Where?" Penny was trying to zip up her suit.

"Just follow me and stay close," he looked out of the window trying to see if someone was outside. Ethan edged towards the door and slowly opened it, the wind came rushing in.

He held his hand up, voices could be heard coming from the direction of the jetty.

"Quick this way," Ethan whispered, Penny followed him out, and they crept along the side of the building, and he pointed towards a path to the left of them.

"Keep low," he whispered, and they ran along the path.

Ethan dragged Penny behind a large rock and peered around. Two men came up the path and stopped when they got outside the building. Penny looked closer and saw that one of the men was Fred, the man who had driven her to the island.

Penny tapped Ethan's shoulder "he is the one who drove me here," she whispered.

Fred slowly took out of his jacket a small gun.

"You go in first," said the other man to Fred.

"Why should I Tim?" said Fred whispering crossly.

"Because you have the gun… numpty," Tim hissed.

"No, you go in," Fred handed him the gun.

"Look Jason will be here soon with the others, and if she is not dead, we will be too," Tim exasperated with Fred and shoved the gun back into Fred's hand.

"Fine, I will do it," Fred sighed and walked up to the door and with an almighty kick, kicked the door. As he did so he lost his footing and fell back and fired the gun, into Tim's leg. Tim fell to the ground clutching his leg, screaming in agony.

"You shot me in the leg you absolute …." Tim was rolling

around on the ground, Fred bent over him and was apologising.

"Let's go," whispered Ethan and they ran up the path.

The came to the top of the cliff. Ethan grabbed Penny by her shoulders.

"If we have any hope of surviving this, I need you to do everything I ask, no questions," he said.

Penny nodded and followed him down the path, she could make out another jetty. It was a very steep climb down; Ethan was constantly looking behind him and beckoned Penny to hurry up. They reached the wooden jetty; the sun was now rising. The sea was a light turquoise colour, the seagulls were swooping around them.

"When we get to the end we jump and swim, luckily the sea is calm," whispered Ethan.

"Ethan I am scared," Penny pulled him back.

"You are not the only one, we will get through this," he gave her a weak smile.

"Going somewhere?" a voice said.

They turned around and standing on the jetty was Olivia, she was wearing a black jacket, with the hood up and black combat trousers.

"Olivia, what are you doing here?" Ethan quickly walked over to her.

She smiled and then from behind a boulder Jason walked out. Penny took a step back. His dark brown eyes pierced right through her. He had shaved off his hair.

"Penny, I see you have been acquainted with Ethan and Olivia," he smiled and slowly walked towards her. Jason tilted his head and then looked her up and down in a menacing way.

"Penny, whatever did I see in you?" He gave Penny a haunting look.

Penny shuddered. He then put his hand out and slowly stroked her face, his hand was rough and smelt of tobacco.

"I like your hair" he whispered and blew her a kiss. Penny closed her eyes momentarily, she felt sick inside.

Jason turned to face Olivia and smiled at her and walked to the edge of the cliff. Olivia moved closer to him and then quickly brought out a gun from her jacket and shot him point-blank in the stomach, and he tumbled into the sea.

Penny gave a shriek.

Olivia turned to Ethan, "He was always so needy and don't get me started with his infidelity, we should never have married," Olivia pointed the gun at Ethan.

"Jason was your husband?" Ethan whispered.

At that point, Fred and Tim came over the hill. They stopped in their tracks when they saw Olivia holding the gun.

"Olivia why are you here?" shouted Fred.

"I asked you two, to do a simple task," she shouted.

"We did as you asked," Fred nervously replied.

"Both of you down here now," Olivia gestured with the gun.

They slowly climbed down the path, Ian hobbling behind Fred.

"Right, kneel," Olivia took a step back from them.

"No Olivia…" Fred whimpered.

"Get down on the floor," Olivia roared.

"Olivia, I can't," Ian said clutching his leg.

Olivia shot him, and he fell back.

Fred looked at Ian, blood seeping from his head. Olivia then shot Fred.

Olivia gave a sniff and turned to look at Ethan and Penny.

"Don't worry you two, I am not going to kill you… yet…I want to drag this out. But first, Penny darling, where are the diamonds?" Olivia gave a quick smile.

"I don't know what you are talking about Olivia…" Penny took a step back from her.

"I think you do… I need those diamonds, now," she whispered.

Penny glanced at Ethan.

"What happened to you, Olivia?" asked Ethan quietly.

She paused before answering.

"Ethan, I was always a loose cannon you know that…" Olivia slowly walked over to him and stroked the gun down his chest.

"You were a successful doctor; how did you get involved with Jason?" Ethan looked down at her with such concern.

"You shouldn't believe what my dear mammy says. She sent me away because unfortunately, I became pregnant…she did not want the shame. I mean it must be awful being a bastard child," she was smiling at Ethan and then gave a wild cackle.

"Who was the father?" Ethan edged forward.

"Oh, don't worry Ethan, it wasn't you. I do not think we ever got to that part. It was someone else," she sighed and pointed the gun at Penny.

"Now Penny, where are the diamonds?" Olivia screamed.

"Olivia, I have no diamonds..." Penny stuttered.

"So Jason was lying...?" Olivia looked down at the ground.

"Yes.." whispered Penny,

"I can't hear you..." Olivia screamed again.

"Olivia, there are no diamonds..." Ethan gave a nervous glance to Penny.

"I was so sorry to hear about Susan," Olivia sighed.

"Ethan, she was such a silly girl getting involved with Jason," Olivia pushed the gun into Penny's side.

"Olivia, what do you mean?" Ethan was now agitated. Olivia quickly turned around and held the gun to her head.

"She didn't commit suicide, darling Ethan. I found out that my dear husband Jason and Susan were together.....It had to end," she smiled to herself.

"Olivia, she took an overdose, she didn't shoot herself," said Ethan now becoming visibly upset.

"I know, but how else was I going to make her take the pills? She took some convincing...quite a little firecracker, she put up a good fight... I will give her that." Olivia began to laugh, she suddenly stopped.

"Her face was a picture with the gun resting against her

temple," Olivia pulled a face.

"You absolute ..." Ethan clenched his fists.

"Oh, stop it, Ethan you never loved her, she knew that. You were always working and the whole island knew she got pregnant on purpose to keep you from leaving her. Every time Jason came back to the island, they were at it. So, we were both made fools of Ethan, I had to stop it."

Olivia directed the gun at Penny's head.

"Right, I think I will shoot you first Ethan; I would like to have a chat with Penny on my own," she turned around and fired the gun.

It jammed, Olivia looked at it, Ethan took his chance and charged at her and grabbed the gun from her and hit her over the head with such force, she collapsed to the ground.

"Run..." shouted Ethan.

Penny ran down to the jetty and jumped into the icy water, Penny heard Ethan jump in behind her. Penny focused on the cliffs in the distance. Ethan was swimming past her. She began to slow down and was taking in too much water and began to choke.

"Come on Penny you cannot stop," shouted Ethan, treading water.

"I am trying Ethan", he swam back and pulled her along. Penny could hear in the distance, a boat. They looked around to check where the boat was coming from.

"That's my RIB," said Ethan confused and briefly stopped swimming. The boat came closer, Ellen and Uncle James were looking in their direction. Ethan waved his arm in the air and Ellen frantically waved back. The boat slowed down and Ellen leaned over the side and helped Penny in. Ethan pulled himself into the boat.

"Ellen your phone now," said Ethan out of breath and holding his hand out. She quickly pulled it from her jacket pocket and gave it to him.

"What are you two playing at?" Uncle James huffed trying to navigate the boat across the waves.

"No time to explain, how did you know where we were?" Ethan scrunched up his looking at Uncle James.

"A little birdie was worried about your insane plan," He said pushing Ethan to one side so he could see.

Ethan called the Coast Guard and spoke to Alan. He asked them to meet him at his house and to stop all the ferries arriving and leaving the island.

"Ethan what the hell is going on?" said Ellen trying to steady herself as the boat sped over the waves.

"If I told you, you wouldn't believe me," Ethan now slid over to Penny.

"Are you ok?" he said hugging her.

"Ethan, is she dead?" Penny pulled back from him shaking with fear.

"Who is dead?" Ellen grabbed Ethan's arm.

"Can we just get back to mine and I will fill you in then," Ethan held Penny and kissed the top of her head. Ellen sat back in the boat and went quiet.

"Uncle James, I want you and Ellen to go back into town and wait at the police station. Penny, I think it would be safer if you stay with me, Ellen who has Sammy?" Ethan turned to look at Ellen.

"Don't worry he is with Mary," she said smiling.

"What!" exclaimed Ethan glaring at Ellen.

"Don't worry, I went over last night to look after him, soon after you left for Moray. Mary came this morning and said she would take him to school and she and Olivia would keep an eye on him. That Olivia is one, she thinks she is so high and mighty," rambled Ellen.

"Will you shut up Ellen," yelled Ethan.

"Hey…" shouted Ellen folding her arms and turning away from Ethan.

"Listen, Olivia is behind all of this with Penny, she was married to Jason … she killed Susan," shouted Ethan.

All the blood drained from Ellen's face.

"Right," growled Uncle James accelerating more.

CHAPTER 12

They came speeding into the bay, Uncle James cut the engine and the boat glided into the jetty. Ethan quickly threw the rope around the jetty pole and pulled the boat in.

They all clambered out of the boat and ran to the steps. Ellen out of breath shouted for Penny and Ethan to go on ahead. Ethan sprinted up the steps and got to the top and punched the code into the keypad. The gate did not open, Ethan tried again, he peered over, and someone had padlocked the gate. He stood back, then ran and barged the gate open with his shoulder.

"Sammy..." shouted Ethan running up the path, Penny quickly followed him. A police car came speeding up the drive. It screeched to a stop, and Alan and another policeman quickly got out.

"Ethan, what is going on?" Alan ran over to Ethan.

"Have you seen Sammy?" yelled Ethan and grabbed Alan's shoulders shaking him.

"No..." Alan shook his head; Ethan pushed him back.

"Sammy," shouted Ethan and ran into the house.

In the hall Mary was lying on the floor, she had blood coming from her head. Ellen came through the door and gasped when she saw Mary and went over to her, and knelt and checked her pulse.

Ellen shook her head and stood up, tears welling up in her eyes.

"This is all your fault," shouted Ethan pointing his finger at Penny, she stood back in shock.

Ellen grabbed Ethan's hand.

"This is not her fault; you need to get a grip," she hissed.

"He didn't mean that," Ellen came over and hugged Penny.

Ethan stormed out of the house.

A faint tapping noise could be heard upstairs.

"Ethan..." shouted Ellen.

Ethan sprinted up the stairs.

"Sammy is that you?" said Ethan standing at the top of the stairs, straining to hear.

"Check the rooms," shouted Ethan, they all split up and went into the rooms.

Penny went into a bedroom and there was a wardrobe, she heard a tapping noise.

"Sammy is that you?" Penny whispered.

Ethan, rushed into the room and flung the doors of the cupboard open. Sitting at the back of the cupboard was Sammy. His feet and hands had been tied and he had been gagged. He seemed to be having a seizure.

"Sammy..." exclaimed Ethan tears welling up in his eyes, he gently lifted him out and laid him down on the floor.

Ellen came into the room.

"I will get his medication and ring for an ambulance," said Ellen taking the phone from her pocket. Ethan quickly untied the gag and untied his feet and hands and rocked Sammy in his arms. Ellen rushed back with his medication and gave it to Sammy. Ethan looked up at Penny, she had never seen someone have so much anger in their eyes.

"He has Epilepsy..." Ellen whispered to Penny.

Penny walked out of the bedroom; in a daze, she walked down the stairs.

Alan came running past Penny and shouted to Ethan.

"We have to go now, there has been a sighting of Olivia," Alan waited outside the bedroom.

"If you think I am leaving him," yelled Ethan.

"Ethan just go; I will stay with Sammy, just go and get that evil woman," Ellen hissed, rocking Sammy.

Ethan slowly walked out of the bedroom and looked down at Penny, their eyes locked. He hurried into another room and came down a few minutes later wearing his uniform. He snatched his policeman's hat from the coat hook in the hallway and then grabbed Penny's arm and whispered "sorry" and pulled her outside.

He marched to the police car.

"Penny, get in the back, Alan, ride upfront with me and John you stay here. Radio us every ten minutes with an update on Sammy you hear," Ethan opened the car door and got in and John ran back to the house.

"Do we get to put the sirens on?" Alan excitedly clapped his hands.

"Hang on," said Ethan and he got out of the car and ran back to the house.

"What is he doing?" Allan whispered.

Ethan came out carrying Sammy "Open the door Alan," shouted Ethan. He slowly put Sammy next to Penny and ran around to the front and sat down.

"I don't know why I didn't think of this before," said Ethan turning on the engine, he flicked a switch and the sirens came on. He swung the car around.

"Alan, can you ring ahead to the Medical Centre and tell them we are coming and mention Sammy's condition. Then I want you to go to the ferry port and wait with Bill. You need to check every passenger," said Ethan tearing down the road.

Penny sat in the back holding onto Sammy and stroking his hair. His colour now starting to come back.

"How is he?" said Ethan quickly looking back at Penny.

"Fine," Penny whispered, trying to smile at Ethan.

They arrived at the Medical Centre and two nurses were waiting for them outside with a trolley. The nurses helped put Sammy on the trolley, Alan ran towards the ferry port and Ethan and Penny followed the nurses, Sammy was coming around.

"Hey, you," said Ethan smiling down at him and holding his hand.

"Dad," he said in a weak voice and then shut his eyes.

"Sergeant Mackenzie we will take over now, you can wait in the waiting room," said one of the nurses and she looked Penny up and down, she was still wearing her wet suit.

They watched Sammy wheeled into a cubicle, Ethan held his head with his hands and kicked a chair, it flew into the wall. A couple of people came around the corner to see what all the commotion was. Penny stood behind Ethan; she tentatively rested her hand on his shoulder. He turned to face Penny.

"I need to get down to the ferry port and wait for the police coming over from the mainland," his eyes darting around "Can I ask you to wait here until Ellen arrives, she shouldn't be too long."

Ethan grabbed Penny's hands and pulled her to him and whispered in her ear "Please forgive me," he pulled back from her.

"Ethan, I am so sorry it is my fault," Penny trying not to cry.

A nurse came up to them.

"Sergeant Mackenzie, Sammy will be fine, a little dehydrated, though, with some rest, he will be right as rain," she said smiling.

She was holding in her hand blue scrubs and a pair of crocs.

"Thought these would be a little more comfortable, there is a room over there you can get changed in," and handed them to Penny.

"Will you be careful," Penny leaned in to hug Ethan and kissed his cheek. Ethan's police radio made a beep.

"Ethan..." the voice crackled.

"Copy," said Ethan impatiently leaning into his radio.

"She is definitely on the island," said Alan frantically.

"Alan?" said Ethan trying to hear him.

"Olivia..." Alan's voice was faint.

"Can you repeat?" said Ethan frustrated with Alan.

"I said Olivia is here, she was last seen running from the beach," Alan now shouting.

Penny pointed to the room opposite, Ethan acknowledged her with a nod and continued his conversation with Alan. Penny opened the door and went in. A few lockers and a bench were running in between them.

She sat down on the bench and put the nurse's scrubs next to her. She looked down at her feet and they were all bloody and covered in dirt. She lifted one foot and looked at the sole of her feet and there were several cuts, with a thorn poking out. Penny noticed some medical wipes in the corner and leaned across to get them and began to wipe the soles of her feet and pulled the thorn from her foot. Penny slowly stood up and took off her dry suit and put the scrubs on.

The door opened, and a nurse came in with her back to Penny she closed the door quietly and turned around.

"Hello," said Olivia and gave Penny a menacing smile and then locked the door.

CHAPTER 13

Penny moved slowly backwards, and Olivia brought out a scalpel and pointed it at Penny. Olivia had blood on the side of her head where Ethan had hit her with the gun. She gestured with the scalpel to move towards her. There was a knock at the door.

"Penny, are you ok in there? Ethan said in agitation.

Olivia quickly moved over to Penny and grabbed her and stuck the scalpel into Penny's ribs. Olivia began to push the scalpel in, Penny felt the tip of the scalpel pierce her skin.

"Yes fine," Penny said through gritted teeth, trying to block out the pain.

"Why is the door locked?" said Ethan and tried the door handle again. Penny didn't answer.

"Are you sure you are, ok? Can you open the door I need to talk to you," he said trying the door handle.

Olivia gestured with the scalpel to open the door and she stood at the side and whispered, "let's be sensible" she took the scalpel to Penny's throat and slightly pushed it in, and Penny nodded frantically.

Penny took a deep breath and slowly opened the door.

"Penny, I have to go, Ellen will be here soon, you will be

perfectly safe," Penny nervously glanced over to Olivia who slowly traced the blunt side of the scalpel across her throat and glared at Penny.

"Yes fine," Penny said quietly.

"Are you sure you are, ok?" Ethan said moving towards her with a concerned look.

"Yes, just tired," Penny tried to close the door.

"Right …bye then and he gave Penny a kiss," Penny broke free from him and Ethan walked back down the corridor.

Penny quickly closed the door.

"Quite the love birds, aren't you?" said Olivia with a jealous tone.

"We will wait five minutes and then we are going to go, put your shoes on now," Olivia demanded. Penny slowly put on the shoes, her feet stinging from the cuts.

"Let's go," Olivia made Penny face the door, pushing the scalpel in Penny's back. Olivia opened the door and nudged Penny forward and she felt the scalpel go into her a little, she let out a gasp.

"Don't be such a big girl," Olivia whispered.

Olivia shoved Penny out of the room and pushed her down the corridor. As they approached the entrance, Ellen came rushing through the electronic doors.

Olivia pushed Penny forward and before Ellen realised who they were, Olivia quickly took the scalpel from Penny's back and lunged into Ellen's stomach and quickly pulled it out. Ellen slumped to the ground. A woman who had been standing by the doors suddenly let out a scream.

Olivia grabbed Penny's arm and pulled her into the car

park. Alec was in a car, he had the engine running and yelled to Olivia to hurry up.

Olivia opened the back door and pushed Penny in the back. Olivia got in next to Alec and screamed for him to go.

Penny quickly sat up in the seat and looked out the back window and saw some nurses attending to Ellen, her body lying motionless.

A sudden rage took over Penny and she leant forward and put her arm around Alec's neck and pulled him to her. He was choking and could not breathe, Olivia dropped the scalpel and frantically tried to find it, Alec was losing consciousness and lost control and crashed into a parked car. Penny was thrown backwards. She went to open the door, though Olivia had already got out of the car, and she dragged Penny onto the road.

"Get up," Olivia yelled; Penny cowered.

Olivia hauled Penny up and again stuck the scalpel into her back and made Penny run towards the main High Street.

Olivia was running incredibly fast; Penny was finding it hard to keep up with her. A man was unloading some boxes from a large white transit van. Still holding onto Penny, Olivia ran up to the man and in the sweetest voice said.

"Excuse me," he turned around and smiled at her, and then with a swiping motion, Olivia slit his throat. There was so much blood, he held his throat and fell to the ground.

"You are pure evil," Penny exclaimed, the blood from the

man had splattered all over Olivia's face.

"I try," Olivia gave a smile, and she wiped her face with her sleeve.

"In now," she roared at Penny.

Penny climbed into the back; Oliva slammed the doors.

The engine started; the van sped off with a jolt. Penny fell into some boxes at the back. She heard police sirens in the distance and what sounded like a helicopter.

Olivia was driving so fast, there were a couple of bangs, which sounded like gunshots and the van slid sideways. The van spun around; Penny was thrown to the side of the van. There was a bump, and the back doors flew open and below Penny, was the sea. The van was balancing on the cliff edge. Seagulls flew past, and a gentle breeze blew around the van. The van was creaking and slowly moving up and down, like a seesaw. Penny slowly moved backwards, and the van suddenly tilted forward. Penny stopped and leant back,she heard cars screeching to a stop and then footsteps running to the van.

"Penny are you in there?" shouted Ethan.

Penny was in shock and couldn't speak.

"Penny," he yelled.

"Yes," she screamed, and the van tilted forward again, she let out a scream.

"We need a tow line on this van now," yelled Ethan.

"Ethan I am going to die," Penny sobbed, she was clutching onto a raised metal plate. She felt herself slipping towards the open doors.

"No, you are not," Ethan shouted, his voice faltering.

"Penny, the tow line will only hold you for a little while, we will have to move fast," Ethan shouted over the noise of a winch.

"There is a sliding door at the side of the van. I am going to open it slowly, though the van may tilt, I want you to be ready and soon as it is open, you are to throw yourself out towards me," he shouted.

"Ok," Penny screamed.

The van tilted downwards, she screamed again, rocks were falling into the sea.

"Ethan, we need to hurry this up, the winch is not holding the van," someone shouted.

"On the count of three, I am going to open the door," Ethan calmly said.

"Ethan I can't do this," Penny yelled, the van dipped down more, and she was sliding further down, the van doors were opening and closing.

"Ethan I am slipping," Penny screamed.

"Is there anything to hang onto "he shouted.

Penny frantically looked to her side and there was a bar running along the inside, Penny eased herself up and grabbed onto it.

"Ok I am holding onto something," she yelled.

"On the count of three, Penny"

"Wait" Penny shouted.

"What?" shouted Ethan impatiently.

"I love you," Penny shouted.

"I would prefer you to say it to my face," Ethan said, his

voice high-pitched.

The tow rope started to shudder, and the van jolted.

"One, two, three…" Ethan shouted.

Ethan slid the door open just enough for Penny to get out. Penny lunged toward him. The van made a groaning noise, and she felt the van sliding down with such force. Ethan pulled her arm, there was a whirling noise from the tow rope, and it snapped. Ethan pulled Penny away from the van and they both tumbled to the ground. Penny quickly sat up and they heard the van smashing against the cliff, there was an almighty explosion when the van hit the beach below. Black smoke billowed upwards.

Penny lay looking up at the blue sky, the seagulls gliding across, a gentle breeze engulfed her, and she breathed in the air.

Ethan began to laugh. Penny slowly sat up and looked down at him.

"What is wrong with you?" Penny said out of breath.

"Oh, I don't know, maybe it's trying to stop a psychopath and pulling you from a van falling off a cliff," he said sighing.

"You are crazy," Penny said smiling.

"I know," he said raising his eyebrows at Penny.

Alan came over; he had a worried look on his face.

"Ethan, can I have a word?" said Alan quietly bending over him.

"Yes Alan, what is it?" Ethan still chuckling.

Alan cleared his throat and then paused.

"Yes Alan, spit it out," Ethan slowly stood up and brushed himself down.

"The Medical Centre has just called through…" Alan again paused.

"Is it Sammy?" Ethan was now concerned.

"No, not Sammy," said Alan shaking his head.

"Well?" Ethan sighed.

"I am so sorry; Ellen she didn't make it," Alan looked down at the ground.

Ethan collapsed to the ground and screamed; he clawed the dirt with his fingers. His face red, Alan stood hovering over him, not sure what to do.

A paramedic came over to Penny and ushered her to an ambulance. Penny was numb and confused and couldn't believe what Alan had just said. The paramedic wrapped a foil blanket around her. Penny watched Ethan walk slowly with Alan to the police car and he flopped down in the passenger seat. Alan quickly ran around to the driver's side, and they drove off.

John, the policeman who had been at Ethan's house earlier came over to Penny. He stood looking at Penny for some time. She looked up at John, his blue eyes full of sadness. He took off his cap and ran his hand through his silver hair.

"John," Penny's lips trembling.

"Yes "he took a step closer to Penny.

"Are the ferries running now?" Penny said staring out to sea.

"They will be soon, why?" he gave a slight sniff and

adjusted his belt and looked up at Penny.

"I am going back home to London; can you drive me to The Lookout?" Penny looked out to sea.

"Well, you will need to give a statement," he said in a fluster.

"I will do it, in London" Penny pushed the paramedic away, who was fussing over a cut on her arm and slowly walked over to his police car.

CHAPTER 14

John ran over to the police car and before he opened the door, he cleared his throat.

"Penny, you have been through hell, though so has Ethan. I have known him for twenty years and ever since you came to the island, he has changed, he has become alive since meeting you and he will need you more than ever now. Can you not stay a little longer?"

Penny got in and put on her seatbelt slowly. John started the engine and turned the car around. He suddenly stopped the car.

"What are you doing?" Penny turned to look at John.

"Penny this is probably going to get me fired, though I have a daughter about your age and if she went through what you have, I would want her safe and sound, home with me. So, I never helped you, you hear? Go get your stuff, I will then drive you to the quayside and you get on that ferry. I will say you gave me the slip if they ask, but I think everyone will just be in shock about Ellen, so we have a little time,"

"Thank you" Penny whispered.

He sped off and pulled up outside The Lookout, Penny quickly ran up the path, tears welling up in her eyes.

She did not have the key, she turned to look at John, and

then ran back to the car.

"Penny?" John frowned.

"I don't have the key.... can we go please?" Penny sighed.

John drove down the road, Penny looked over her shoulder, The Lookout disappeared out of view.

He pulled into the quayside and nervously looked around "Go" he whispered.

Penny ran in the direction of the port. There were two ferries, she ran up to a man who was wearing an orange High Vis jacket.

"Excuse me when does the next ferry leave?" Penny said out of breath.

"Oh, about twenty minutes, you will need to board now though, just show me your ticket," he said looking Penny up and down, wearing her nurses' scrubs.

She had no money, she held her hands over her face in desperation.

John quickly ran up behind her and gave her twenty pounds.

"Here take this" he shoved the money into her hand.

"I can't "Penny cried.

"Penny, get on the ferry," he said and pushed her towards a kiosk, cars were starting to go up the ramp.

While Penny was waiting to buy her ticket, she saw John talking on his police radio, he had a concerned look on his face.

Penny got her ticket and walked over to where foot passengers boarded the ferry. A lot of people came up behind her and pushed her along.

Penny heard John calling her name, she turned around, the man behind her pushed her along. Penny got to the top and looked over the side of the ferry.

The engines started, and John was on the quayside, waving his hands at Penny, shouting something. She leaned forward to try to hear what he was saying, though she couldn't hear him over the engines.

The walkway had now been winched up. John went over to some of the crew on the quayside, he seemed desperate. They ignored him and another man in a High Vis jacket came over to him.

The ferry moved sideways and glided out of the port. Penny watched the island slowly disappear and sadness took over. Penny looked down at the turquoise sea.

Suddenly the boat made a groaning noise, and she felt the boat slow down and it seemed to be turning around. A few of the passengers started to walk over to the railings, there was confusion as to why they were turning around. Then the captain spoke over the intercom to the passengers.

"Due to a security alert, we are to go back to port. There is no need to be alarmed," he said in an annoyed tone.

A couple next to Penny gasped and started to move away from her. Penny turned around slowly and there was Olivia, her face and clothes covered in blood. Her arms were battered and bruised, and she was holding a knife.

Olivia limped towards Penny, holding out the knife and with her other hand holding her rib.

"Penny, you really have nine lives, don't you?" she said

wincing with pain.

"Olivia, you were in the van, you went over the cliff?" Penny stuttered.

"Not quite, I jumped before the van lost control," she said through gritted teeth, in pain.

Two of the ferry crew ran over and stopped when they saw Olivia with the knife.

"Penny, come with me," she winced and limply waved the knife at Penny.

"No" Penny shaking her head.

"Penny stop being so difficult and do what I say," Olivia screamed.

"Why Olivia, why bring me up here?" Penny shouted, there was a crowd now gathering around them. One of the crew turned his back on them and was talking on his radio.

"Jason stole the earrings from me, do you know how much they are worth?" Olivia gasped, holding her ribs.

Penny shook her head.

"A lot...I need them, so where are they?" Olivia said through gritted teeth.

"I don't understand why you didn't kill me?" Penny took a step back.

"Penny, I needed to know where they were," Olivia held the knife up, the blade glinted in the sunlight.

"Olivia, hand yourself in, you need medical attention," Penny stood her ground.

"No," she said again in pain, she was turning pale and

sweating.

"Did you really kill Susan, or was that to wind up Ethan?" Penny nervously looked at her.

"Seriously these questions. Yes, I killed her, Ethan was better off without her. Can you just move towards me, it would help a great deal..." she said holding her ribs and bending over, blood seeping through the material and dripping on to the deck.

"Now..." she roared.

Everyone on the deck moved further away from them.

Then with a shriek, Olivia ran at Penny with the knife. Penny moved out the way and Olivia fell to the ground and slid against the railings. Penny moved forward and Olivia grabbed hold of Penny's leg. Penny turned around and kicked Olivia's shoulder.

She was still holding onto Penny. With all her might Penny kicked the knife from her hand. It flew across the deck and a man gingerly bent down and was in two minds to pick it up.

"Grab it.." Penny shouted at him.

Penny hauled up Olivia by her shoulders and pushed Olivia against the railings. Olivia's eyes were flickering, she was losing consciousness.

"I do have the earrings, and this is for Ellen," Penny hissed and pushed Olivia over the side.

Penny looked down and saw Olivia's body floating face down, her red hair floating around her. Everyone on the deck ran over to have a look.

The ferry came into the port and standing on the quayside were Ethan and some police officers. The crew lowered the walkway, and Ethan quickly jumped onto the walkway. Penny watched as the crew were escorting the passengers off and Ethan pushed past them.

He reached the deck and slowly approached Penny.

"Were you not going to say goodbye?" He was out of breath and seemed annoyed with Penny.

"I was..." her lips started to tremble, and tears slowly rolled down her cheeks.

Ethan looked out to sea, there was now a RIB coming across the bay.

Penny walked over to Ethan and took his hands in hers and looked up at him.

"Ethan, I am so sorry about Ellen; I am to blame," Penny said crying.

"No not at all," Ethan pulled Penny close to him and kissed the top of her head.

"How is Sammy?" Penny rested her head on his chest.

"He is fine and will stay in the hospital tonight, just as a precaution. I must go back to the station, we have Alec in custody, and I must interview him. I could get John to run you back to The Lookout, also this is a big ask, but my house is still a crime scene. Could I stay at yours?"

"Of course, no problem," Penny whispered. Ethan handed his mobile phone to her.

Penny looked at him blankly "phone your parents" he said smiling.

Penny took it from him and desperately tried to remember their number.

"What?" Ethan tilted his head.

"I don't know it," she whispered and looked down at the floor.

Ethan smiled with his eyes and pulled her towards him.

"And this is why I love you," he whispered, he quickly let go of Penny and looked upwards biting his bottom lip.

Someone called his name; he turned and held his hand up to acknowledge them.

"Penny, come back to the station, we can find the number there."

Penny paused before following him.

"Come on," he beckoned her to follow him.

A car came screeching into the quayside, the driver's door flew open, and Jimmy ran over to Ethan and Penny. His eyes were red and puffy. He was ranting at Ethan, making no sense.

"How could you let it happen?" he screamed at Ethan.

Ethan looked shocked and couldn't answer him. Ethan held up his hands as if to try and calm him down.

"And you," he pointed at Penny, his eyes glaring.

"You are pure evil; you are the reason my darling Ellen is dead. You killed her, she was sweet and caring," he fell to his knees, sobbing.

He then wiped his eyes and stood up.

"You were trouble, the first time I laid eyes on you. It should be you in the mortuary not Ellen," he screamed at

Penny.

"Hey...Jimmy, enough!" shouted Ethan and tried to grab his arm.

"Oh, you would protect your little tart," he swiped Ethan's hand away.

"Jimmy, it wasn't my fault, Ellen was a beautiful person..."

Jimmy marched up to Penny.

"Shut up, you do not have the right to speak about Ellen. She did not deserve to die; you should have died," He yelled again.

Rage took over Penny.

"If you hadn't been playing around and showed her the respect she deserved, you two would probably be serving together right now in the pub. Ellen died the day she found out about you and Jean, she loved you so much," Penny screamed.

Jimmy was silent trying to process what Penny had just said. Penny caught Ethan's eye and he looked away from her.

Ethan walked up to Jimmy and put his arm around him and guided him slowly back towards the police station. Ethan didn't even turn around to look at Penny. The crowd dispersed and John walked over to Penny.

"Come on Penny," he said softly.

"John, I think I will wait here until the next ferry goes," Penny said with a sigh.

"Fine, probably best," he nervously looked over at Ethan.

"John, I have left my bag at Ellen's," Penny started to cry, and she frantically ran her hands through her hair.

"I tell you what when the dust has settled, I will ask one of the lads to pick it up, though it is still raw for everyone, so just give me a little time and I will send it to you," he rested his hand on her shoulder.

"Thank you..." she whispered.

"It will be ok Penny and in time...." he stopped himself.

Suddenly some of the crew ran up the walkway of the ferry and a man in a High- Vis jacket ran past John and Penny.

"What's going on Ian?" called John, to the man.

The man turned around and shouted "Change of plan, we are going back to Oban now to collect passengers and then will come back here for the crossing tonight,"

"Ian..." called John.

"Yes John," said the man impatiently.

"Do you have room for a wee little one... think she deserves it?" he said smiling at Penny.

Ian looked at Penny.

"Oh, go on then...." beckoning Penny and continued to run up the walkway to the ferry.

John pointed at the ferry "Go on then."

Penny gave him a quick peck on the cheek and leaned into him.

"Thank you, John, I will pay you back when I get home," Penny stepped back and ran towards the walkway. She stopped briefly and looked around the quayside. She pulled herself together and boarded the ferry.

The ferry set sail, and one of the cabin crew, a young girl came up to Penny and handed her some trousers and a blue jumper.

"Here you are, Ian asked me to give these to you," she said staring down at Penny.

Penny smiled at her and sat on the deck holding the clothes and staring at the island now disappearing.

CHAPTER 15

Four hours later they arrived in Oban, Penny wearily walked down the ramp to the quayside. There was a pay phone in the car park. Penny opened the door to the phone box and took a deep breath. She picked up the receiver and dialled the operator.

"Operator," a woman said crisply.

"I would like to make a reverse charge?" Penny said, biting her thumbnail.

"Which number please?"

"I will give you the address..." Penny said.

"Please hold..." there was a click and then Penny heard her mother's voice.

"Mum..." Penny burst into tears and leaned against the side of the phone box.

"Penny is that you, where are you?" her mother frantically asked.

"I am in Oban and I have ...." Penny couldn't breathe.

"Penny deep breaths, just talk slowly," her mother calmly said.

"I need you to come and collect me, I have no money."

"Fine, book yourself into a hotel and we will fly up tomorrow first thing," she went quiet "Penny what happened?" Her mother sighed.

"I will tell you tomorrow," Penny whispered.

"Ok well just call me and let me know the hotel, dad will pay...." she went quiet.

"Mum, are you there?" Penny was trying not to cry again.

"Yes, Penny I am just so glad to hear your voice, your dad would speak to you, though he is crying his eyes out," she said laughing through her tears.

Penny wandered into Oban, she walked into the first hotel she came across. She opened the door to the hotel. It had a tiny reception area, under some stairs. Penny approached the reception desk. The receptionist was looking down at a file, scratching her head with a pencil. She wore thick-rimmed glasses, her hair was wild and curly, and she was wearing a very overpowering perfume mixed in with stale cigarette smoke.

Penny coughed, the receptionist looked up and smiled, and pushed the file to the side. The computer screen reflected off her glasses.

"Good evening," The receptionist smiled. Penny stared at her and noticed her name badge, said Ellen, Penny couldn't take her eyes off the badge. The receptionist quickly looked down at her name badge and tilted it. Penny looked up and gave her a quick smile.

"I need a room, single is fine," Penny looked around the reception.

The receptionist quickly typed on the keyboard and sat up "you are in luck, we have one left, otherwise you would have had to have the deluxe room and that is quite pricey," she said giving a little laugh.

"Can you fill out your details and do you have any luggage?" she picked up a card and placed it in a holder and handed it to Penny.

"Sorry are you ok?" said the receptionist with genuine concern.

"I will be..." Penny slowly picked up the card, the receptionist hit the bell next to her, and Penny jumped. A young porter came running downstairs.

"Andrew room twenty-four please," said the receptionist, with a smile.

The porter showed Penny to her room.

"So, business or pleasure," he said, quickly walking down the corridor.

"What?" Penny mumbled.

"Are you here on holiday or have you come for business?" he was smiling at Penny.

"Neither..." Penny said in a daze.

He frowned at her. They stood outside the room, and he put the key card in, it buzzed and opened the door.

"Breakfast is served between seven and nine o'clock."

He was still hovering by the door; Penny walked in and closed the door. She looked around the room, through the white net curtains she could faintly see the port. Penny walked over and lifted the curtain. The sea was a dark blue, with storm clouds in the distance. Penny wandered into the small bathroom and turned on the shower and stood in front of the mirror and looked at herself, mesmerised by the steam misting up the mirror.

"Penny get a grip, you are safe now," she clutched the sink

and hung her head.

She quickly undressed and stepped into bath and pulled the damp curtain along and sat down and curled up. The water splashed over her body. She lay watching the water swirling around the plughole.

Her thoughts turned to Ethan. How could he be so cold to her? She pushed herself up and brought her knees up to her chest.

"He said he loved me..." she whispered.

She finished her shower and walked into the bedroom and switched the television on. It was the local news with the ticker at the bottom saying *"Terror on Stonray.* A picture of Ellen flashed up, then Mary and the delivery driver. Then there was a picture of Olivia and Jason. The newsreader then mentioned that Alec had been charged with several offences.

She switched off the television and lay on the bed exhausted and fell into a deep sleep.

Penny awoke the next morning, the clock on the radio said eight o'clock. She put the jumper and trousers on and went down for breakfast. Everyone in the breakfast room turned to look at her. A waiter came over and showed her to a table. Penny looked across and a man was reading a newspaper and the headline read *"Massacre in Paradise."*

Penny sat down at the table, and everyone started to talk again.

"Would you like, coffee or tea?" said the waiter, rearranging the table.

"Coffee please," Penny nervously brushed her trousers.

"Right you are, breakfast options are on the menu..." he

looked around at the table for a menu.

"Oh, let me get you one," Penny put her hand out to stop him and shook her head.

"Just toast please," she whispered looking down at the table.

"Right you are," he said in a cheery tone and walked over to some more people who had entered the breakfast room.

Penny looked around the room and now and again someone would look over at her.

Then a man came into the breakfast room. He was wearing a suit. He saw Penny and walked over to her. Penny panicked and placed her hand over the knife.

He sat down "Penny Brown?" he said taking out a notepad. Penny didn't answer.

"You poor thing, absolutely terrible what happened to you, can I get a comment?" he gave a concerned look.

"Are you a journalist?" Penny's paranoia kicked in. She wasn't sure if he was one of Jason's men.

"Yes, Daily Record, so tell me in your own words what happened?" he said looking around the room.

"No comment," Penny said firmly, moving her cutlery around in agitation.

The waiter came over.

"Can you please leave?" he said to the journalist.

"You won't know I am here; I am not bothering anyone?" he gave Penny a quick smile.

"Please leave, you are bothering one of our patrons," the

waiter said through gritted teeth.

"So, Penny did you witness the killings, were you there?" he brought out a Dictaphone and shoved it under her chin.

"Now," said the waiter annoyed and waved to one of his colleagues to come over.

"Ok," said the journalist, holding his hands in the air, he took a card out of his top pocket and placed it in front of Penny "Call me if you change your mind."

The waiter pointed at the door, and the journalist left.

"Your toast will be here very soon," said the waiter and walked off and then turned to Penny. "You are very brave" he whispered and picked up a Newspaper and placed it down on the table in front of her. Penny pushed the paper to one side, everyone looking at her and whispering.

The toast and coffee arrived, and Penny forced herself to eat some of the toast and leaned back in her chair. She could not eat, she felt sick, and her head was throbbing.

Penny placed the napkin down on the table and walked out. As she was passing the reception she realised, she hadn't told her parents which hotel she was in.

Penny decided to ring her sister. She asked the receptionist to look up her sister's law firm. Penny ran up the stairs to her room, she dialled the number and waited. A woman answered the phone "Baker Stone Associates" she said in a brisk tone.

"Can I speak to Annabel White please?" Penny's voice trembling.

"Yes, who is calling please?" she sighed.

"Her sister…"

The woman went silent.

"Hello, are you still there?" Penny asked desperately.

"Of course, yes, sorry I will put you through now," her tone anxious.

Penny was put on hold. Greensleeves was playing.

"Penny," shrieked Annabel, Penny held the phone away from her ear.

"Are you ok, it is all over the news, what the hell happened, where are you? Mum and dad have been so worried, of course I was worried about you. I always said I didn't trust Jason," she took a deep breath.

"Annabel, I need you to ring them and tell them I am at the Castle Hotel, it's on the High Street in Oban" Penny calmly said.

"Penny…" Annabel cried hysterically.

"Annabel please don't cry; you will set me off," Penny lay on the bed.

"Penny, it has been all over the news, did you know the people murdered?" Annabel whispered.

"Annabel, I will see you when I get home, just call mum and dad."

Penny stayed in her room, anxiously waiting for her parents, and the phone rang.

Penny leaned over and picked up the phone.

"This is reception, you have some guests," The man said.

"I will be down soon," Penny leapt off the bed and hurried out of the room. She ran down the stairs. She looked down into the reception area and she could see her parents huddled in a corner, whispering to each other. Her father looked up; a smile crept across his face. Her mother quickly turned around.

"Penny," her mother screeched.

Penny's mother was tiny, she never had a hair out of place, and her appearance was always immaculate.

Penny approached her mother; her mother frowned.

"Mum," Penny whispered.

"My darling, we are so glad you are safe.." Her mother looked up at Penny, she still was frowning.

"Mum, what's wrong? Penny sighed.

"Nothing..." her mother looked around.

"Has something happened?" Penny tilted her head.

"What have you done to your hair?" Penny's mother whispered.

"Beverley, this is not the time..." Penny's father stepped forward and flung out his arms. He hugged Penny tightly.

Penny's father was very tall, and thin. Electric blue eyes, white hair. He stood back from Penny, tears welling up in his eyes "I am so glad you are safe" he took a deep breath to calm himself.

They took the train from Glasgow. Penny sat in silence the whole journey. Her parents tried to talk to Penny, though she would shut them down. They eventually arrived at her parent's house in Surrey at midnight.

Over the next few days, Penny would stay in her room most of the time. Her parents had been in the same house for the last forty years. Though it did not seem like home.

The press camped outside their house, much to the annoyance of her parent's neighbours. Though by the end of the week, Penny was old news and they moved on to someone else's misfortune.

Penny was sitting at the kitchen table one morning and her mother came in.

"Right, we are going to have a little party on Saturday," she said in a cheery voice.

"No mum, I need to get back to my flat and have some normality," Penny flicked through a magazine.

"I know, but please don't rush things, stay as long as you want. I spoke to your work, and they have said take all the time you need," she was frantically looking for something in a cupboard.

"So, can we, have it?" her mother turned to look at Penny.

"Have what?" Penny looked up at her mother.

"The party, in fact, let us just have lunch. Annabel and family and maybe some others?" she said casually.

"Fine whatever, but I am going back to my flat," Penny said firmly and left the room.

Saturday came around. Penny sat in the sitting room, watching her father filling the bowls with crisps. He was very gentle. Her parents were not exactly a perfect match height-wise. Though they loved each other, still head over heels in love forty years later. Her thoughts then turned to Ethan. Now she was back she was in two minds if she should contact him.

The doorbell chimed; her father walked to the front door.

She heard her sister. Penny's nephews charged into the sitting room and stopped when they saw her. Annabel walked into the room and looked at Penny and burst into tears, holding her arms out and hugging Penny.

"I am so happy to see you, though what on earth have you done to your hair?" she stood back frowning at Penny. Annabel like their mother was immaculately turned out. Long blonde hair, slight tan and slim. She was taller than Penny.

Everyone stood around talking. Now and again, Penny caught concerned looks from her sister and mother. Though no one mentioned what had happened. It was as if, they could not comprehend it themselves.

Lunch was served and Penny sat at the table, watching everyone chatting away. She felt her life had stopped.

"I can't do this; I can't do this…" Penny stood up.

Everyone looked up at her.

"Penny," said her mother slowly.

"Sorry, everyone I just can't sit here anymore, I need to go, dad can I borrow your phone?" Penny said frantically.

"She has gone mad," said Annabel whispering to their father.

"I have not gone mad, Annabel, I need to see Ethan," Penny slowly sat down in her chair.

"Ethan," they all said looking at each other.

"Oh, you wouldn't understand," Penny shouted.

Penny walked into the kitchen, and everyone followed her.

"Will you calm down?" said her father trying to make

Penny standstill.

The doorbell then chimed again.

"Bill whoever it is, tell them to go," shouted Beverley.

Annabel and Beverley watched Penny frantically opening cupboards and draws.

Penny's father came back into the kitchen.

"Penny there is someone here to see you," he said quietly looking towards the front door.

"Who?" said Penny slamming a drawer shut.

From behind her father, Ethan walked into the kitchen.

CHAPTER 16

"Hi," he said softly. Everyone was transfixed.

"Why are you here?" Penny whispered. Ethan nervously looked at everyone.

"Out everyone," Penny's father ushered them out of the kitchen.

Annabel craned her neck to look at Ethan.

Ethan walked slowly over to Penny.

"You haven't just come to do a statement have you?" Penny said flustered.

"No, I haven't," he said smiling.

Penny looked up at him. He took her hands and looked down at her.

"Penny, I want you to know that I do not blame you for Ellen's death. You must believe me. Can we please just start again?" he pleaded.

"Ethan, I want you more than anything, you know that. But how can we have a relationship when I am down here and you up on the island?" Penny said resting her head on his chest.

"Come back with me," he said pulling away from her, his eyes smiling.

Penny leaned against the kitchen cabinet and tapped her hands together.

"Next week is Ellen's funeral and I would like you to be there… actually I need you to be there," His eyes were full of sadness.

"How can I go back, after everything that has happened?" Penny now pacing around the kitchen. Ethan gave a little laugh and shook his head.

"Penny can you just take a breath and at least think about it? I think if we can get through the trauma, we both experienced, anything else will be a walk in the park, don't you?" He said raising his eyebrows.

"Yes, but won't Sammy find it difficult? He went through so much that day and then to throw me in the mix is not fair on him," Penny sighed, clutching her hands together.

"Ok maybe moving in with me straight away might be a little on the crazy side … how about if ……" Ethan paused

"Yes," Penny moved closer to him, her eyes darting around.

"I am not one to be impulsive and please do not think I am mad and crazy, but would you consider…actually no I can't say it…" he was in a panic and was holding his hands over his face.

"Ethan," Penny stamped her foot in frustration. He took in a big intake of breath and then exhaled.

"Would you consider moving into Ellen's flat and possibly taking over the shop?" He turned his back and rested his hand on the counter. Penny walked over to him and put her arms around his waist.

"I would be honoured too, though Uncle James and

Jimmy, may think differently?"

The kitchen door moved slightly. Penny walked over to the door and quickly opened it. Annabel gave an embarrassed look "sorry" she whispered. Penny closed the door on her.

Penny turned to look at Ethan. He was deep in thought looking out of the kitchen window. She turned Ethan around to face her.

"Uncle James is fine about it; I sort of mentioned it to him the other day and Jimmy leave him to me," he kissed the top of Penny's head.

"Actually Ethan, I can't..." Ethan's face dropped, and he moved back.

Penny leant on the counter and looked at Ethan, he folded his arms and forlornly looked down at the floor.

"Can I live with you?" Ethan turned around quickly "As you said anything else will be a walk in the park." Penny felt a rush of excitement.

"Of course," he pulled Penny towards him.

"And the shop?" he looked down at Penny.

"One day at a time..." Penny whispered.

Ethan was invited to stay for lunch. Her father and Ethan talked nonstop about boats. Annabel and her mother organising Penny's life.

Ethan was going back to the island the next day and Penny agreed to go back with him. She handed in her notice at work, and it was decided that Penny would rent her flat. It would give Penny an extra income if she decided not to take on Ellen's shop.

This time Penny packed properly to the dismay of Ethan. He was not happy having to wheel five suitcases.

The family promised to visit at Christmas. Penny was apprehensive about going back to the island, though, with Ethan by her side, she felt she could do anything.

Arriving back on the island was bittersweet. Penny was with Ethan and excited about what lay ahead. Though the sadness of the events still haunted her. She gazed at the white beaches, the sky a silver-blue. As they passed The Lookout, Penny shuddered.

Penny knew she would always be an outsider on the island, though, in time, she hoped she would be accepted. On the flight up, Penny decided that she would take on Ellen's shop on one condition, that the name was changed.

They pulled into Ethan's driveway and Uncle James opened the front door and slowly walked out. He was not the man she met a couple of weeks ago. He looked frail, his face ashen. Penny got out of the car and looked around. Ethan threw the cases out of the car shaking his head.

"Penny dear," Uncle James said softly and hugged her.

"Mr Mackenzie" Penny replied.

He pulled back "Uncle James," he said trying to smile. He turned to Ethan, who was kicking a suitcase.

"Ethan, Sammy is at school, are you able to pick him up?" Uncle James said with a slight wobble in his voice.

"Yes of course," Ethan slammed the car door and almost tripped over a suitcase.

"Good, well I will be going now," Uncle James pointed to his car.

"See you, Penny, I have to go to the Kirk to organise the funeral," he broke down in tears.

Penny looked at Ethan, not knowing what to do.

"Uncle James, would you like me to go with you?" Ethan walked up to him and rested his hand on his shoulder.

"Would you, I can't do this on my own," breaking down again.

"Of course, let me take in the many suitcases," said Ethan, rolling his eyes at Penny.

Uncle James gave a little laugh at the suitcases spread all over the drive. Ethan dragged a suitcase and was swearing as he did so.

"Penny," said Uncle James quietly.

"Yes," Penny said softly.

"Probably not the right time to mention it, though sometimes there is never a right time. Did Ethan mention Ellen's shop to you?" his lips trembling.

"Yes, he did, and I would be honoured to take it on. I owe so much to Ellen, and I will carry on her legacy. Though I will take it on, on one condition?" Penny folded her arms.

"What's that?" He was fiddling with his car keys.

"We change the name to *Ellen's*," Penny leant in and smiled.

"That would be just perfect, I will get it changed tomorrow," tears rolling down his cheeks.

For the next few days, Penny settled into the island. The

shop's name was changed, and it was decided that the shop would re-open after the funeral.

The day of Ellen's funeral came. They all sat around the kitchen table, Ethan thought it would be best if Sammy went to school, he had been through too much lately. Sammy and Penny managed to strike up a friendship. Penny's mother said to her before she left. Be Sammy's friend, not his mother and then it should all fall into place.

It was time to go, and they followed the hearse in Ethan's car. The service was taking place at a small chapel on the headland. Outside a man was playing the bagpipes. The chapel was too small to hold everyone, so those who were not family stood outside. The whole island was there, over a hundred people.

Penny sat next to Ethan; she looked around the chapel. It had been filled with Ellen's favourite flowers; the smell was intoxicating. A picture of Ellen rested on the altar. At one point, the chapel doors opened, and Penny glanced over her shoulder. A man was standing at the back of the chapel, he did not look like a local, though he looked familiar to her.

After the service, they went back to the village hall. Everyone seemed sombre at first, though when the whisky had been opened, it livened up. Penny was sitting at a table and Jimmy came over to Penny, with two glasses and a bottle of whisky. He placed a glass in front of her.

"Penny, can we talk?" leaning over and pouring whisky into a glass.

"Yes of course," Penny was a little nervous about what he was going to say.

"You and I have something in common," he said swirling the whisky around his glass.

"Do we?" Penny said with a surprised look.

"Yes, we do..." he downed his whisky.

"We have Ellen. I now realise that you were a true friend to her. She didn't have many friends and even though you both only knew each other for a very short time, I like to think that your friendship meant the world to her, that she knew she had a true friend, a kindred spirit if you like," he began to cry, his body shaking up and down.

Penny stood up and went over to him and put her arm around his shoulder.

"Come here Jimmy, Ellen meant the world to me, I am so sorry for all those things I said,"

Jimmy tapped her hand.

"Let's start afresh and anytime you want to get away from grumpy over there... as we know he can get very grumpy..." Jimmy laughed through his tears, pointing at Ethan, "Please come into the pub and have a drink with me," he sighed, wiping the tears from his eyes.

"Of course," Penny looked over at Ethan, he looked back to her and mouthed "what?" Penny smiled at him.

Jimmy got up with the bottle of whisky and took a swig out of it and stumbled towards the bar in the corner.

Penny was about to go over to speak to Ethan when John came over.

"Penny," he said and gave a quick smile.

"John, lovely to see you again. I owe you twenty pounds still," Penny opened her bag.

"No put it away, buy me a few drinks, now you are friends with the landlord," nodding at Jimmy who was now been helped to a chair by a couple of men.

"Fine…" Penny smiled at him.

"Anyway, just thought I would come over and say hello and can I just say thank you and goodbye," he said.

Penny frowned at him.

"Yes, I am retiring and moving to be closer to my daughter in Inverness and to thank you for coming back. Ethan is a changed man. You know…. not so…" he paused.

"Not so grumpy…" Penny looked over at Ethan.

"Exactly," he said holding up his finger.

Ethan came over to join them and John made his excuses and left.

"You have quite a little fan club, don't you?" said Ethan raising his eyebrows.

"Do I?" Penny smiling at him.

"You know you do, what were you talking about?" he said now taking her hand.

"You," Penny flicked his chest.

"All good I hope…" Ethan puffed out his chest, his eyes smiling.

"Of course," she said and kissed him.

Ethan pulled Penny close to him "We will have to go soon; I have my new boss starting tomorrow and I need to impress. It will be weird having to report to someone," Ethan sighed.

"Is he a local?" Penny pulled away from him.

"No from the mainland and from all accounts difficult," He rubbed the side of his face, with his hand.

CHAPTER 17

For the next few weeks, Penny threw herself into learning how to run a shop. It was hard, though she loved being her own boss. She made very subtle changes and made sure the shop was still Ellen's. It gave her a chance to form her own relationships with the locals. Penny suggested to Jimmy that he advertised the pub in the shop, so tourists knew about the pub. By all accounts, his takings doubled in the first week from when the sign was put up.

Ethan would come home most nights in a foul mood because of his new boss. When Penny tried to talk to him about it, Ethan would shut her down. Penny was beginning to think that moving in with Ethan may have been a big mistake.

One night he was in a particularly bad mood. He came into the kitchen and sat at the table. Penny was busy with dinner. He was tapping the table and then stood up.

"Bad day...again," Penny said rolling her eyes.

"Yes actually," he was sounding like a petulant child.

Penny turned to the drawer and took out some cutlery and threw it on the table. The back door opened, and Uncle James walked in whistling. Ethan glared at him and stormed out of the kitchen.

"Ignore him," Penny waved her hand and set the table.

Uncle James went to sit in a chair.

"Well, you two need a night out, I will mind the bairn and you go and talk to that grumpy so and so." He rubbed his face with his hands.

"Are you sure?" Penny rested her hand on his shoulder, he nodded and took out his phone.

Penny went to find Ethan, she passed the sitting room and Ethan was standing at the window, looking out at the sea. The sunlight rippled on the waves. It was early August and there was a hazy autumnal feel. He turned around when Penny entered the room.

"Sorry," he said forlornly.

"Uncle James has agreed to mind Sammy, so go and change and we are going to the pub," she leant on the sofa.

"I don't know why you want to spend time with me," he threw his hands in the air and flopped down on the sofa.

"Come on, get your glad rags on..." Penny held her hand out to him and he looked up at her and smiled. Penny pulled him up and watched him walk out of the room. She went back into the kitchen.

"All ok?" Uncle Jimmy was leaning on the counter and looking at his phone. Penny nodded and went to the back door and took her coat down and slowly put it on.

"Uncle James can I ask you something," Penny slipped her hands into her pockets and slowly walked to the table.

"Yep anything," he was looking down at his phone bringing it close to him and squinting.

"What was Susan like?" Penny whispered.

He turned with a surprised look.

"Well…. we didn't know her to be honest. Connie my wife, knew her better. She was trouble from the start. Ethan and Connie were close and when Connie died, Ethan was heartbroken. Susan did not even come to the funeral, because she had booked an expensive Spa weekend on the mainland. They should never have got married," he huffed.

"And his birth parents?" Penny was still looking down at the floor.

"My lassie, you are full of questions…difficult ones too," He scratched his head.

"All I know is that they were from the mainland. My brother, William never spoke to me about it. Why all these questions?" He moved closer to Penny.

"Oh, I don't know. I just feel maybe that Ethan is suffering from delayed PTSD. It is quite common, after trauma, which may explain the constant bad moods," she trailed off.

"PT What?" Uncle James sniffed and looked blankly at her.

"Sorry, Post-traumatic stress disorder. I trained as a clinical psychologist. Trauma was my forte," Penny sighed.

"Wow, I never knew that about you. Ethan said you worked in PR," he scrunched his face up.

"Yes …I did," Penny went to sit at the table.

"Why the change?" He sat down next to her, intrigued, his eyes wide.

"Money," Penny stood up and went to get a bottle of wine and two glasses.

"So, what do you do, as a psychologist?" He leant back in his seat. Penny passed his glass of wine, and he rested it on his rather large tummy.

"Well, I trained and then got my doctorate. My first job was at a prison," Penny looked down at her hands.

Ethan walked into the room "Who was in prison?" he said pulling his collar up.

"Penny," Uncle James quickly said. Ethan squinted his eyes at Penny.

"It's not what you think..." she said smiling.

"She is a thingy... a .... Shrink," Uncle Jimmy exclaimed.

"Really?" Ethan came closer to Penny.

"Clinical Psychologist...was," she tapped the table and did not look at Ethan.

"Doctor?" Ethan said putting his phone in his pocket.

"Well ..yes," Penny replied.

"Whoop we have a doctor in the family," Uncle James slapped Penny's back. She fell forward.

"Shall we go, Doctor Brown?" Ethan said with a smile. Penny nodded and they walked to the car in silence.

"Is this our first date?" Ethan rested his hands on the car roof.

"I guess it is," Penny opened the door.

"Are there any other things I should know?" Ethan got in and put the key in the ignition and glanced at Penny.

"Nope...you know everything now." Penny looked out the car window and could see the town along the coast, the lights twinkling. Penny had to be patient with Ethan. He had, had so much upset in his life recently. She had to stop analysing everything and learn to relax.

They arrived at the pub, there were a few cars parked outside and they walked in. Jimmy was serving at the bar and acknowledged them with a wave. It was certainly livelier, since the first time Penny was here.

Penny went to sit at a table and took her coat off, Ethan was chatting to Jimmy. She looked around the pub and noticed, that Jimmy had given the room a facelift. The walls were painted a cream colour, the chairs and tables had been painted a lovely soft grey and hanging on the wall were Ellen's paintings. Penny took a deep breath, desperately trying not to cry.

Ethan came over and took a packet of crisps out of his jacket pocket. He sat down and took a sip of his beer.

"Cheers," Ethan said, tight-lipped, holding up his pint.

Penny acknowledged with a nervous smile.

"Ethan, you seemed annoyed..." Penny whispered leaning forward. He shook his head.

"Ethan," she knocked on the table to get his attention.

"Sorry, I am adjusting. I feel I know you, though we have only known each other for just over a month and ...." He looked down at the table and moved his stool closer to her.

"The feelings I have for you are scary," he made a strange face. Penny sat back in her chair and flipped the beer mat and sighed. More people came into the pub and the noise was beginning to make Ethan more agitated.

"Ethan, you have lost three very dear people in quick concession. You are bound to be feeling sad, upset, and angry. Though if you are having any doubts about us, you must be honest and tell me now and I will leave."

Ethan grabbed her hands and leaned into her. "No, you have me for life," he smiled with his eyes. Penny shyly looked down at the table.

"So, tell me, if there was any place in the world, you would love to go to, where would it be?" Ethan sat back in his chair, he lunged forward "Hang on let me guess…India?"

"No, have been…" Penny gave a weak smile.

"Hmmm, Brazil?" he tapped the table with his finger.

She shook her head.

"Where then?" He scrunched up his face.

"Please don't laugh, or think I am weird," Penny squirmed around in her chair.

Ethan leant forward "where?" he whispered.

"Disney World," Penny winced.

"Disney World…that is a peculiar choice… but hey…" he shook his head smiling.

The door to the pub opened and a woman dressed in a long white jumper, skinny jeans, and high heels walked in. She had long blonde hair extensions, a deep tan and was very tall. Behind her, a man came in. Penny's face dropped, Ethan noticed this and turned around.

"Oh Jesus, this is all I need," Ethan was shaking his head. Penny tensed up. The couple walked to the bar and the man shook Jimmy's hand. Ethan looked at Penny and then the man.

"Penny?" Ethan waved his hand in front of her face; she was in a trance. The man turned around and noticed

Penny and he quickly turned away.

"Do you know Michael?" Ethan sat up and tilted his head.

"Yes," she whispered and looked down. Michael and the woman went to sit at another table, Ethan gave him a wave and Michael nodded.

"What is going on?" whispered Penny. Sitting back in her chair.

Ethan looked over at Michael and the woman.

"Michael was Jason's best friend. I spent a week skiing with him." Penny frantically ran her hands through her hair. Michael got up and walked over to them.

"Small world, good to see you again Penny," Penny turned away from him.

"Not too late tonight, Ethan, need you on top form tomorrow," Michael tapped Ethan's shoulder.

The woman came over and stood next to Michael and smiled at Penny.

"Kat, let me introduce you to Ethan and Penny." Michael presented her like a trophy. She smiled.

Michael leant forward, "From Estonia, doesn't speak the lingo" He chuckled.

"Was Jason into Sex trafficking as well?" Penny folded her arms and sat back in her chair. Michael stopped laughing and scowled at Penny. Ethan was mortified. Michael walked back to his table.

"Come on let's go," Ethan downed his pint and stood up.

They walked back to the car, both deep in thought.

"Ethan, you need to find out what is going on, Michael is

up to something," Penny whispered.

The next day Penny arrived at the shop; she was deep in thought. Jason and Michael were thick as thieves, always out together, never left each other's side. She looked over at the police station, in two minds if she should confront Michael.

She took the keys from her bag and tried to find the right key. There were thousands crammed onto a hoop. She rested her hand on the shop door and it opened slightly. She frowned, looking at the door slowly opening and gently pushed the door and walked in, the bell ringing above her.

She covered her face; the shop had been ransacked. The paint had been poured over the shelves and walls, and food was all over the floor. A cold feeling took over her body. The door opened, and Jimmy walked in. Penny turned and looked up at him, his face in shock.

"What the hell?" he whispered looking down and stepping over some paint on the floor.

"Wait here, I am going to see Ethan," Penny marched over to the police station, anger now taking over. Alan was sitting at the front desk, flicking rubber bands at the wall and sighing. He looked up when she marched up to the counter.

"Penny," he said cheerily. She marched straight past him and lifted the countertop.

"Hey" Alan stood up and followed Penny. Michael was talking to a policeman, laughing, and sipping a coffee. His face turned sour when he saw Penny.

"Why Michael?" Penny shouted. Ethan came out of an

office. Michael looked at Ethan and sighed.

"Alan, why is a member of the public in our office?" he shouted.

"Oh, stop deflecting Michael, I know you were behind trashing Ellen's shop," Penny fled out of the station. Ethan ran after her. Penny crossed the street and stopped.

"Penny, what has got into you?" Ethan demanded, his eyes darting around.

Penny grabbed his arm and pulled him into the shop. Ethan gasped, he looked at Jimmy, who was picking up some of the food off the floor.

"Jimmy stop," Ethan rested his hands on his head and turned to Penny.

"Penny, it's kids, did you lock the door last night?"

Penny turned away from him and defensively folded her arms "Of course I did," she hissed.

Alan came rushing in "Hells bells, what has happened here?" tiptoeing around the paint on the floor.

"Chief wants to see you, Ethan," Alan nervously tapped Ethan's shoulder.

"Penny we will come over later and help clear up." He sighed and ushered Alan out.

"It is not kids," Penny hissed and took her coat off and rolled up her sleeves and went to the back and came out with a brush. She scanned the room, not knowing where to start.

Jimmy made his excuses and left and promised he would come back later to help. Penny began to sweep the floor. She heard the bell ring "we are closed" she sighed with her back to the person.

Penny heard footsteps walk up behind her. She stopped sweeping and slowly turned around; Michael was standing in front of her.

CHAPTER 18

He took off his cap and tucked it under his arm and surveyed the room, tutting.

"Ethan will be back any minute," Penny nervously took a step back from him.

He shook his head slowly from side to side.

"Ethan has gone on an errand for me, and won't be back for ages," he leaned forward and smiled at her. Michael walked over to the door and turned the lock, sighed, and slowly turned around. Penny edged backwards and tightly held onto the broom.

"Boo," he said waving his hands and laughing.

"Penny are you scared of me?" he edged forward and then stamped his foot, and she jumped.

"Why are you here Michael? Could you not cut it in London?" Penny gave him a quick smile. She curled her fingers tightly around the broom handle.

"Jason is dead, he can't protect you. I used to think how pathetic it was the way you followed him around. Yes, Jason, three bags full Jason…" Penny narrowed her eyes.

Michael lunged forward and tried to grab her. She managed to step out of the way, and he slipped on some paint onto the floor.

"Whoops," Penny said raising her eyebrows. There was a knock at the door, Penny heard her name called, it was Uncle James.

"Coming," as Penny walked past Michael she stepped on his hand deliberately, he cried out in pain, clutching his hand.

"Get out," Penny pointed at the door, Michael slowly got up, covered in paint,and holding his hand, Penny unlocked the door.

Michael leaned into Penny "Just remember Penny ...they never found Jason's body," he hissed. He put his cap on and Penny opened the door and he pushed past Uncle James.

Uncle James looked back at Michael, with paint down his back. Uncle James came into the shop and gasped when he saw the mess.

"Jimmy said it was bad, though I didn't think it would be this bad," He rubbed his chin slowly with his hand. He made a beeline to the counter and walked to the back and thundered up the stairs. Penny followed him up to the flat. He was looking around, opening cupboards, he even looked under the bed.

"Uncle James?" Penny followed him into the kitchen. He stretched upwards and took down a laptop, above the kitchen cabinets.

"A few weeks before you arrived on the island, Penny had installed CCTV cameras. One of those fancy things, you can watch on your phone or laptop. We can see who the culprit is," he gave a quick smile.

He went downstairs carrying the laptop and looked

around the room. He pointed to a small camera above the counter, mounted on top of a stag head and rested the laptop on the counter and pressed the *on* button and waited for it to power up. Penny peered over his shoulder. It prompted for a password, he was biting his fingernail, trying to think what it might be. He typed something and it did not work.

"Here let me have a go," Penny took a deep breath and typed slowly on the keyboard, and the home page flashed up. Penny stood back.

"What did you type?" he said smiling.

"Tarty Jean," Penny raised her eyebrows.

"Oh Ellen," he said chuckling and then he began to cry.

Penny rubbed his back "Let it out," she whispered.

"It hurts so much." He stood back from her and looked upwards, desperately trying to pull himself together.

"Look why don't you go home; you need time to yourself."

He nodded his head and wiped the tears from his eyes.

Penny was still clearing up the shop, late into the evening, desperately trying to get the shop ready for tomorrow. She looked around, paint still on the floor, the shelves empty. Even though Ellen had a particular style, it didn't bring in many of the tourists, just the locals. Penny sat down and made up a list of what needed to be changed. She looked at the books and realised that gifts and confectionary were the most items bought.

The bell rang and Penny looked up and Ethan walked in.

"I saw the light on," he walked up to the counter and leaned over and kissed her. Penny shuffled her lists together and put them in her bag.

"What are you going to do, the place is a state?" folding his arms and resting on the counter.

"I have an idea, though need to run it past Uncle James," she picked up her bag and held her hand out to Ethan, and pulled him towards the door. He flicked the switch by the door.

"Who is looking after Sammy?" Penny exclaimed.

"He is at his friends," he said nuzzling her neck.

"You are in a good mood," she leant back from him.

Penny locked up; Ethan leaned over her shoulder "Had some good news today," he said kissing her neck.

She turned to look at him, he stood back from her.

"Michael is leaving..." He whispered and looked over in the direction of the police station. Penny pulled on the door, to check it was locked.

"He has been here less than a month..." she said scowling at the police station.

"I don't care.." he said with a grin.

Ethan punched the air in excitement and did a little skip. They walked to his car, and he zapped the car, the lights flashed and he suddenly stopped.

"You have to be kidding me..." he walked over, all his tyres were flat.

"Ethan, did they find Jason's body?" Penny quietly asked.

Ethan was crouched down looking at a tyre.

"What....?" he scrunched up his face.

"Did they find Jason's body?" Penny whispered, looking

around.

"No, they didn't," Ethan was preoccupied with his tyres.

"All four of them..." he groaned.

"Ethan, the shop, now your tyres, this is not some kids," Penny said sharply.

Ethan looked around and rubbed his chin.

"They are not connected," and kicked a tyre.

"I am calling your uncle to pick us up," Penny took out her phone, and Uncle James turned up ten minutes later and drove them home.

Ethan and Uncle James were chatting away. The moonlight, dappled on the dark sea. A wind had picked up, the rain lightly falling.

Penny became more wound up, suddenly she blurted out "Ethan we need to look at the security of your house."

He turned around and frowned at her.

"Penny what has got into you?" Glaring at her; Penny glanced at Uncle James.

"It's something Michael said," Penny whispered and clutched her bag.

"What did this Michael say?" Uncle James looked at Penny, in the rear-view mirror.

"He said they never found Jason's body..." Penny looked out of the car window.

"Jason is dead, he would never survive that fall, the gunshot or bobbing around in the sea. The forensic boys did a thorough job. He will probably wash up on a beach in Orkney or Ireland. You were spooked seeing Michael, but he is going now."

Penny shook her head in disagreement. They turned into the drive. The sea was crashing against the rocks, the wind was blowing over the car.

"Looks like there is a storm coming, you two better get in,"

As soon as Uncle James said that, the heavens opened. They made a dash for it.

Uncle James wound down his window and shouted.

"I will come by tomorrow and take you both in," Ethan was trying to find his keys; Penny raised her hand. The rain was blowing sideways, they could hardly stand up. Penny walked in and switched the hall light on, it didn't work. She tried another switch.

"Great the fuse has blown, or the storm has knocked out the power," Ethan huffed, a huge flash of lightning lit up the hallway. Ethan reached up on the shelf by the front door for a flashlight and switched it on and they walked down to the kitchen.

"I just wanted a hot bath," Penny stamped her foot and threw her bag down. Ethan took the flashlight and held it under his chin and made a sound like a ghost.

"Such a child...I am going to light the fire, it's freezing," Penny wearily walked into the sitting room and put some logs on the fire and stood up to find some matches.

The power came on and the light from the hallway flooded the room. Penny stopped in her tracks. On the round table by the bay window, all the photographs had been replaced by pictures of Jason.

Penny quickly walked into the kitchen, Ethan was

standing by the AGA and was pouring some wine into glasses. He turned to look at her, she could not get the words out. She beckoned him to follow her, he slowly put the wine bottle down and followed her back into the sitting room. Penny pointed at the round table. Ethan stepped forward and turned to look at Penny.

"Please don't say kids did this," Penny whispered.

Ethan put his finger up to his lips and pointed upstairs. He grabbed her hand and took the poker from the fireplace. They slowly walked to the foot of the stairs, Ethan peered upwards and held his hand up to Penny and pointed he was going up the stairs. Penny shook her head "I am coming with you" she whispered and held his hand tightly.

They crept up the stairs, it was pitch dark. Ethan stood still to see if he could hear anything. There was complete silence, only the sound of the wind howling around the house. There was a flash of lightning and thunder, and they both jumped. Ethan pushed the bathroom door open, and it creaked as he did so. He quickly checked behind the door. He came out and they made their way through the rooms, checking cupboards, and under beds. They stood on the landing; Penny was trembling. Ethan took his phone out of his pocket and placed it to his ear.

From Sammy's room, there was a bang, Ethan crept down the landing and placed his hand on the door, it swung open. The window was open, and the curtains were blowing in the wind. Ethan raced to the window and peered out. He could hear footsteps running across the gravel. Ethan thundered down the stairs and flung the front door open and rushed across the lawn. Penny close behind him. He stopped and threw his phone at Penny.

"Ring the station and tell Alan, to send Charlie and Andrew up here and he needs to ring the Serious Crime Task Force and speak to DS William Jefferson, and get him to call me." Penny was desperately trying to remember his instructions. She looked through his phone for the number. The rain was pouring down, the wind almost blowing her over. Alan answered the phone. Penny explained the situation and relayed Ethan's message. Penny got off the phone and looked around for Ethan. She made her way towards the gate. Ethan came running from the other direction.

"They have gone," he said out of breath.

"Ethan, what is going on?" Penny frantically looked around.

"Let's go back to the house and wait for Andrew and Charlie. First thing tomorrow we are getting a proper security system, I agree it is not safe." He put his arm around her shoulder and guided her back to the house.

CHAPTER 19

Charlie and Andrew turned up fifteen minutes later, and Ethan took them first into the sitting room.

"Ethan, what the hell?" Andrew looked down at the photographs of Jason.

Penny walked into the sitting room "Hi guys..." she said bringing her cardigan around her.

"Penny..." they both said distracted by the photographs.

"Did Alan get hold of DS Jefferson?" Ethan asked.

"Afraid not, but he will no doubt call you when he gets the message," Charlie came closer to Ethan.

"Could be kids?" Andrew stepped back from the table.

"It is not kids...Ellen's shop, Ethan's tyres, and this?" Penny snapped.

"Has Michael left the station?" Ethan asked.

"Aye, he has..." Andrew looked at Ethan.

"Where does he live?" Ethan walked to the door.

"He has gone, got a ferry this evening..." Andrew looked around the room.

"Convenient..." Penny sourly said.

"Look, Ethan, it could be someone with a grudge. My advice is to beef up your security and we will do a sweep of the area." Charlie gave a heavy sigh.

"A grudge, no, whoever did this is linked to Jason, can you not get someone to come and dust the photo frames and try and get some evidence?" Penny pulled at the sleeves of her cardigan.

"Maybe get a dog as well?" Andrew folded his arms and looked at Ethan.

"No, I am not getting a dog, "Ethan shook his head.

"Shame..." Andrew sighed.

Ethan frowned at him.

"It's just when we got the call from Alan, we were at Ian Wallace's, he came across a stray. I know it doesn't belong to anyone on the island." Andrew blew out his cheeks.

"Where is the dog?" Ethan looked at them.

"In the car," Charlie gave a quick smile.

"Ethan, can I have a word?" Penny pulled Ethan to one side.

"Look, can we at least think seriously about this. A dog is a start, I will feel safer."

Ethan closed his eyes and clenched his fists.

"Charlie, Andrew, what is the dog like?" Ethan sighed; Penny tapped her hands together in excitement.

They both looked at each other.

"What is wrong?" Ethan turned to look at them.

"Nothing is wrong, come and have a look..." Andrew beckoned them to follow him.

They followed them out, the rain had stopped, Andrew went to the passenger door and opened it. Penny and

Ethan peered in. Penny squealed in delight.

"Oh, my you are so cute," she bent down, there was a brown puppy." It licked her face.

"I thought you said it was a dog…that thing won't protect us.." Ethan hissed.

"Ethan, I don't care, this puppy is so scrumptious…" Penny walked back to the house.

"Well, we will leave you…" Andrew and Charlie quickly got into the car.

"Charlie, Andrew come back here now…" Ethan shouted, he looked back at the house, Penny had gone in with the puppy.

Ethan walked into the kitchen; Penny had already made a bed for the puppy from a cardboard box.

"Penny is this such a good idea?" he looked down at the puppy fast asleep.

Penny turned to him.

"Rex is small now, but he will grow… and judging from his paws, he is going to be big.."

Penny smiled down at the puppy.

"Rex.." Ethan sighed and pulled Penny to him "Who will look after him when we are at work?"

"I will …he will come to the shop with me. Ethan, I don't feel safe on my own, and when you work nights, being in this house, with just Sammy and I can be scary at times. We are so isolated here."

"Fine on one condition though… you change his name," Ethan smiled with his eyes.

"To what? "Penny gave him a quizzical look.

"Bear...he looks like one..." Ethan gently stroked the puppy's head.

"Fine, Bear it is..." Penny whispered.

The next day Ethan got a call from DS Jefferson, he wasn't as helpful as Ethan had hoped. From all accounts, all of Jason's associates had gone underground. Penny threw herself into getting the shop up and running. Over the next few months, life returned almost to normal.

A month before Christmas, the shop was busy with customers and Penny was frantically serving. A man came in and walked up to the shelves, Penny glanced at him, though didn't pay any attention to him.

Bear was in his basket asleep behind the counter, he was only four months, but he was the size of a small Labrador, the vet said he was a cross between Newfoundland and St Bernard, Bear was going to be huge.

The bell rang again, Penny felt overwhelmed, she looked down at Bear and gave a heavy sigh, another ferry was expected in the next hour. Her takings had shot up since she had started to cater for the tourists. She served a customer, watched them leave, and craned her neck, to see if she could see the next ferry coming in.

Penny noticed the man standing behind a shelf staring at her, he made her feel uncomfortable. There was an old lady on the other side of the shop, looking through the tartan rugs and pillows.

The man took an item from the shelf, still looking at Penny. She bent down slowly and stroked Bear. He sat up and shook his head and gave a yawn and stood up and walked around the counter.

"Oh, my what a dog," the old lady said and wandered over to him.

Bear cocked his head and went up to the old lady wagging his tail.

"Some guard dog you are," Penny whispered to herself, nervously glancing at the man, who was now walking around to the far end of the shop.

"My son has a Newfoundland, lovely breed," the woman said stroking Bear's head.

The man came out from around the shelf. Bear looked at him, he began to growl at the man. The woman stood back from Bear.

"Sorry he is normally so quiet," Penny held onto his collar. Bear was barking furiously; Penny was struggling to hold him. The man quickly left the shop.

The door closed, and Bear stopped barking, gave a little yelp, and went back to his basket.

"Well he was told..." the old woman said laughing and came over to the counter with her basket.

After the old woman had left, Penny quickly locked the door. She was in two minds if she should tell Ethan.

"Penny, get a grip, Bear only barked at the man...her paranoia, was becoming a problem.

An hour later, the ferry had docked, and it seemed half of the ferry had descended into the shop.

Penny had a line of customers waiting to be served.

Ethan,came into the shop with Alan, and they pushed past the customers. Ethan took his cap off and went behind the counter and stood next to Penny and rolled up his sleeves.

"What are you doing?" Penny whispered and moved him to the side so she could get to the till.

"Well, if you don't want my help," Ethan held his hands up and was about to walk away. Penny pulled his jumper "Ethan, sorry please help…" she groaned.

Alan came over and leaned on the counter "I don't remember it ever being this busy," he said looking around.

"Alan, don't just stand there, come and help us," Ethan throwing his hands in the air.

Alan helped to pack, and Ethan and Penny served customers.

"Penny, can you pass me the machine," said Ethan holding his hand out. Penny put her hand down on the counter and handed him the machine, Penny was deep in thought about the man earlier.

"Penny that's a stapler," said Ethan frustrated and leaned over and got the card machine. The first thing Penny did when she took over the shop was to get a contactless card reader.

The next ferry came in, they all looked at each other and the door once more opened. The ferry passengers looked a little confused as to why policemen were serving behind the counter.

"You need to get more staff," said Ethan frantically trying to use the machine.

"I know," Penny hissed.

Eventually, there were only a few customers left. They patiently were waiting in line when Ethan suddenly dropped down on one knee.

CHAPTER 20

"What have you lost?" Penny said giving a customer their change.

"Nothing," Ethan said looking up at her, Alan came in between them, to get something from the counter.

"Alan will you just move," said Ethan pushing Alan's legs.

"Hey, watch where you are putting those hands," said Alan and gave a little squeal.

Alan stood back from Ethan "Ethan what are you doing down there?" Ethan glared at Alan.

"Ok I will move," Alan stepped over Ethan and almost knocked him over in the process.

Ethan cleared his throat "Penny" he said quietly.

"Yes," Penny now looking down at him.

"Will you marry me?" Ethan asked smiling.

Penny was stunned, all the customers were now peering over the counter looking down at Ethan and then looking at Penny, waiting in anticipation for her answer. The shop fell silent.

Penny stood back and nearly fell into Alan.

"Yes, of course" Penny exclaimed, Ethan, stood up and pulled Penny to him. The shop erupted into cheers.

Penny's parents were thrilled and of course, so was Uncle James. As Penny's family were coming up for Christmas, they thought they wouldn't waste any time and get married on New Year's Eve.

Her parents flew up a week before Christmas, to help with the planning. It was a whirlwind. Every day was spent, organising the wedding, or running the shop. Penny was exhausted. Annabel and her family were arriving the day after Boxing Day, as they had to spend Christmas with her in-laws. They arrived after a fourteen-hour journey. It had started to snow a little in the afternoon, there was a light dusting on the ground.

Annabel got out of the car "Wow this house is amazing" she said looking around. Penny's nephews Freddie and Richard were asleep in the back of the car. Freddie was around Sammy's age and even though they were not cousins, Penny hoped they would get on.

Her parents had kindly agreed to open the shop and she would pop down later. With New Year the tourists were still coming to the island, and it would be a shame to close it.

After everyone had been shown around, the boys were introduced to each other, Sammy took the boys up to his room and Annabel and Penny went for a walk.

Bear came with them.

Annabel hated dogs; she would flinch every time Bear came near her.

"You have done well," said Annabel staring out at the sea.

"Thank you... I think... you sound almost jealous," Penny said looking at her.

"No, I didn't mean it like that, I just meant, considering how your life was six months ago," Annabel glanced at Penny.

"Well, I do have to sometimes pinch myself," Penny said kicking a rock into a flower bed.

"Tell me, how does Ethan manage to afford a house this size on his salary?" Annabel pursed her lips together.

"Annabel," Penny exclaimed and shook her head.

Though six months ago Penny would have asked the same question. With Penny it was all about material possessions and how much boyfriends earnt and how many holidays she could get out of them. Now she is content and even though she craves a good cup of coffee and a manicure she wouldn't swap her life for anything now.

The next couple of days became even more hectic and Ethan seemed distracted. Penny didn't want to bother him, so she didn't pry. One night he was even more distracted and not himself. He returned from his shift and was clattering around the kitchen. Everyone was in bed, Penny came into the kitchen and sat down at the table stretched her arms out and yawned.

"By the way, Sammy and Freddie have hit it off. They are now roommates, won't leave each other's side," Penny said to Ethan.

"Right good," he said not looking at her.

"Ethan, what is wrong?" Penny said now sitting upright in her chair.

"Nothing, probably wedding nerves," he said looking down at the floor.

Penny slowly stood up.

"You don't want to get married, do you?" Penny quietly said.

"Oh, I do, believe me, I do," he said raising his eyebrows.

"Well, why are you extra grumpy at the moment?" Penny defensively folded her arms.

"Sit down," he said with a slight sigh and pushed her back down in her chair.

Ethan paused.

"I had a call from a police colleague in Glasgow," Ethan took his phone out of his pocket.

"DS Jefferson," Penny quietly asked, a coldness transcending through her body.

"Yep.." Ethan took out his phone and placed it on the table.

"And…" Penny nervously asked.

"He was concerned that there had been a lot of activity with Jason's old gang and wanted to know who was running the show, as to speak, so he asked around" Ethan tapped the table with his finger.

Ethan cleared his throat and sat upright.

"It seems Jason's father is now running the gang and is operating from Glasgow, not south London. He has also made a few visits over here in the last few months, according to Ds Jefferson," Ethan rubbed his face.

"To see Alec?" Penny said quickly.

"No, he has been moved to the mainland," Ethan shook his head.

Penny's blood ran cold and then it became clear to her.

"Penny, what is it?" Ethan gave her a concerned look.

"I have seen him," Penny said clutching her hands.

"Seen who?" Ethan stood up.

"His father, he was at Ellen's funeral and also he came into the shop the afternoon you proposed". Penny said feeling scared.

"Really"? Ethan narrowed his eyes.

"Yes, I just felt he was familiar, and I couldn't think why and now it makes sense. I had met him before, the night at Jason's party. He was introduced to me as Frank, by one of Jason's friends. What if it is retribution. His son was killed?" Penny said panicked.

"Yes, but by Olivia, not us," said Ethan desperately.

"Still, we survived and that won't make a difference to him, no he is here to make trouble, I can feel it, it's like he is trying to spook us. He must have been the one who trashed the shop, your tyres, and the photographs," Penny chewed her thumbnail.

"Your imagination is going to get the better of you," he said poking her shoulder.

"Come on bed, last night before the real dramas start," he said resting his hands on her shoulders and gently rubbing them.

The next day was manic, flowers arriving, dresses delivered, food cooked. The reception was going to be at the house, as they only had close family, Jimmy, and some of Ethan's work colleagues. Penny's friends from London couldn't make it, due to the short notice. Though in the

Spring, her parents were going to have another party, so family and friends could celebrate then.

Ethan was staying at Uncle James that evening and Sammy was going with him. Annabel was Penny's maid of honour and John was Ethan's best man. Ethan wanted Jimmy, but Jimmy had a habit of getting too drunk and Ethan couldn't risk Jimmy's best man's speech.

The morning of the wedding came around too quickly and before Penny knew it, she was getting ready. Her mother did her hair and Annabel did her makeup.

Once they were ready, Penny walked down the stairs, her father was standing at the bottom. He let out a gasp and began to cry. Which set her mother and Annabel off. Once everyone had stopped crying, they got into the cars and made their way to the chapel, where Ellen had her funeral. It was blowing a gale and freezing. Penny held out her hand, her father gently took it and squeezed her hand. Penny smiled up at him and they walked to the chapel doors, she could see into the chapel, the glow of candles, it looked so magical.

Ethan was standing at the altar, wearing his kilt. John turned when Penny walked down the aisle, he gave her a warm smile and turned to face the front. Ethan waited until she was level with him before he turned to look at her. Ethan gazed down at Penny and took her hands. She smiled up at him, remembering the first time they met. How rude he was, she smiled to herself.

"What?" Ethan mouthed.

"Love you" she whispered and held his hands tightly.

The vicar pronounced that they were husband and wife and they kissed, and everyone stood up and clapped.

Penny and Ethan arrived back at the house first. Ethan ran around to the passenger door and opened it.

"Mrs Mackenzie," he said with a grin.

"Why thank you, dear husband..." Penny gave a laugh.

Ethan picked up Penny.

"What are you doing?" squealed Penny.

"Carrying you over the threshold," Ethan was struggling to hold her.

"Put me down..." Penny protested, he gently put her down and rubbed his back.

Cars were coming down the drive, Ethan pulled Penny quickly inside and closed the door. He took from his jacket an envelope and handed it to her.

She looked up at him.

"Open it before everyone comes in.." he looked over her shoulder.

She ripped open the envelope, there were two plane tickets, she looked at them.

"Oh my.." her eyes became wide.

"You are going to Disney World baby..." Ethan picked her up and kissed her, she slowly slid down and began to cry.

"Hey, I thought you wanted to go there?" He stepped back from her.

"I do...ignore me...I think the emotions of today are catching up with me." Penny fanned herself with her hand.

The doorbell went, and Uncle James was shouting for them to open the door.

Ethan opened the door, and they all came through to the sitting room. Penny's mother and Annabel brought the food out, Uncle James serving the drinks. Jimmy turned the music up, and the celebrations began.

It was coming up to midnight, and most of the guests had gone.

"Right Alan let's get Jimmy home," John leaned over Jimmy, who had passed out on the sofa.

Alan didn't answer John and went over to get himself another drink.

Ethan clapped his hands, everyone turned to look at him.

"Right, everyone, please can I ask that you all leave, my wife and I..." Ethan was interrupted by Alan.

"Ethan, can I have a word..." Alan became agitated and downed his whisky.

"Alan no, Ethan and Penny need time on their own. Now, help me get Jimmy into the car." John protested.

There was an almighty crash from the kitchen.

"What the hell..." Ethan stormed out of the sitting room, Penny picked up her dress and quickly followed him.

Ethan approached the door and stopped.

"Penny wait there..." he whispered and cautiously peered into the kitchen. Penny ignored him and came up behind him and looked in.

The back door was swinging back and forth, the wind had blown over glasses.

Ethan walked further into the room. From behind the kitchen door, two men grabbed Ethan and dragged him out.

John and Uncle James came rushing in.

"Penny, what has happened?" John exclaimed.

"I don't know, two men grabbed Ethan, we need to go after them..."

They turned, Alan was blocking the kitchen door, holding a gun.

CHAPTER 21

"Right, this is what will happen, I will leave here with Penny. No one is to move. Do I make myself clear?" Alan yelled.

"Alan.." whispered John and took a step closer to him.

Alan fired the gun and John slumped to the floor.

Alan pushed Penny out of the kitchen and pulled her down the hallway.

"Penny you are driving…" He gave her a shove and pushed her towards his car.

Alan opened the driver's side. Penny slowly got in and put on her seatbelt. Alan was pointing the gun directly at her, and then ran around to the passenger door and got in.

"Now drive to West Point beach," Alan pointed the gun at Penny's head.

Penny turned the key in the ignition.

"It's always the quiet ones…" Penny muttered and reversed the car.

"Now Mrs Mackenzie, I do not want any smart alec comments from you, Jason needs the diamonds."

"I knew it…. where has he been hiding… oh let me guess Moray…" Penny said hitting the steering wheel.

"Where are they? "Alan pushed the gun into her shoulder.

"Alan, I will give them to you when they have released Ethan."

"Not going to happen..." Alan said through gritted teeth.

"Listen, if Jason wants them, he must let Ethan go. Tell them to meet us at West Point beach." Penny hissed.

"Shut up shut up..." Alan thumped the window with his fist, and Penny flinched.

"Alan, how did you get involved with Jason? What hold does he have over you because you are not exactly gangster material?" Penny hissed at him.

"Penny, the less you know the better..." Alan sighed and moved the gun up to her head again.

Penny was approaching West Point beach, she looked down and noticed that Alan was not wearing his seatbelt. She accelerated.

"Penny slowdown...." Alan frantically shouted.

She got up to sixty.

"Ok," she slammed on the brakes, the car skidding, Alan flew forward, and his head hit the windscreen with such force that it cracked. Penny brought the car to a standstill. She leant over, Alan's face was covered in blood and she prised the gun from his hand and raced down to the beach. She could make out in the distance a boat coming across the bay.

It began to pour with rain, the waves crashing along the beach. A hand covered her mouth and dragged her backwards.

"You shouldn't have done that," Penny looked upwards,

Alan's face covered in blood.

She tried to break free.

"Penny stop," he held her tighter and took the gun from her.

Penny looked to her side, a figure was walking towards them.

"Hello Penny," Jason said with a menacing smile.

"Now Penny darling, those diamond earrings, are mine. So, let's end this, so I can leave this cold horrible island.." Jason gave a quick smile.

"Jason, we have company..." Alan nodded to the boat, now coming into the bay.

Jason grabbed Penny and dragged her along a path, dunes were on either side.

"I have to say, Penny, I didn't think you would wear such an elegant wedding dress, I thought you would go for something sluttier."

Penny turned away from him.

"Penny, tell me where they are..." Jason hissed in her ear.

"They are on Moray, I buried them..." Penny looked back at the boat, she desperately tried to see if Ethan was on it.

Footsteps could be heard running behind them. There were a couple of shots fired, Jason stopped and looked back at the beach. Alan was lying on the ground.

Jason brought out a gun and waved it around, pulling Penny up the path.

A man jumped down from the dunes above them, and Jason tensed up.

"Carlos is that you?" Jason stuttered.

"Yeah, I know, I have lost almost four stone…" He said tapping his stomach.

"Carlos, Penny stole the earrings from me, I will have them for you soon." Jason pleaded.

Michael appeared from behind Carlos, smirking.

Jason hung his head.

"I should have guessed…" Jason sighed.

"Listen no hard feelings, but Carlos pays better." Michael tilted his head and gave a smile.

"So, the diamonds where are they lady?" Carlos grabbed Penny's arm, and Jason pulled at Penny.

"Michael," Carlos clicked his fingers.

Michael came behind Jason and pointed a gun to his head.

"Bye Jason…" and fired the gun, Jason slumped to the ground, blood seeping from his head onto the white sand.

"Right ladies first…" Carlos pointed a gun at Penny and pulled her across the beach to a waiting boat.

The speedboat raced across the sea, they slowed down when the island came into view.

"I want to see Ethan…." Penny said desperately.

"You need to be calm, little lady, he is safe on that boat," Carlos pointed to a boat moored to the jetty.

Penny was taken along a path, up to the cliff's edge.

"So where did you bury them?" Carlos gave a smile, exposing a gold tooth.

"In there…" Penny pointed to a building.

"Where, in there…" Carlos snarled.

"Show me, Ethan, is alive and I will tell you," Penny took a deep intake of breath.

Carlos nodded to Michael, Michael brought out a radio and spoke to someone.

Penny looked down and saw two figures come onto the deck. Penny looked closer; she saw Ethan in his kilt.

"You see…" Carlos smiled.

"I lied…" Penny frantically said.

"Come again?" Carlos sniffed.

"Ethan has them, he wanted me to wear them, when we returned to the house, for the reception."

Carlos gave a smile and then slapped Penny across the face.

"You are not to make a fool out of me," He screamed.

"No one is going to have those earrings, you will regret ever saying that Penny," a voice said. Frank came from behind a boulder. He walked closer to them holding a gun, in the other hand, he was holding something.

"Frank…" Carlos exclaimed.

Frank lifted his hand "Look Penny…" he nodded his head at the boat.

And pressed his thumb down, and the boat which Ethan was on exploded.

Penny let out a scream and fell to her knees.

A helicopter flew over their heads, it swooped down and hovered over them, and a light shone down.

"This is the police, you are surrounded, put the weapons down,"

Penny looked up and Frank, the gun pointing down at her.

"Now go and join Ethan, Penny," Frank hissed.

A shot was fired, and Frank fell backwards.

"Put your arms up to where I can see them," a man's voice said.

Penny slowly raised her hands, she looked to her side, and several armed policemen were running towards her. She looked down at the boat on fire, she couldn't breathe and screamed out Ethan's name.

ONE MONTH LATER

Ethan's body was never recovered, and Penny was inconsolable.

Michael and Carlos were arrested. John had luckily survived.

A memorial for Ethan took place two weeks later. The whole island gathered on the beach, to say goodbye to Ethan.

Penny's parents, Jimmy, and Uncle James supported her the best they could, though as the weeks rolled on, Penny became withdrawn.

She would spend most of the time in her room or she would take Bear for long walks on her own. Her parents stayed on and helped as much as possible with Sammy and the shop.

One day Penny returned from a walk, she passed the kitchen and overheard her parents talking. She stood outside the door listening.

"Beverley, we have to be cruel to be kind," her father sighed.

"I know, but it is too soon to leave her. She is barely functioning." Her mother hissed.

Penny pushed the door open, and they both looked at her.

"Penny, dear come and sit," her father ushered her to a chair. Penny slowly walked over and flopped down.

"Penny, we have been thinking, it might be best if we leave, give you and Sammy, some space," her father said gently.

"I am not staying here," Penny said curtly folding her arms.

"Penny, you need to stay, your life is now, here with Sammy," Her mother said firmly.

"No, it's not, he is not my son." Penny glared at her mother.

"Penny, I know you are grieving, but that little boy has lost his mother, father, and Ellen. He needs you." Her mother hissed.

"Not my problem..." Penny turned away from her.

"Well, we are leaving tomorrow, so I suggest you pull yourself together and stop wallowing in self-pity. You only knew Ethan for five minutes," Her mother snapped.

"Beverley, that is way below the belt," Penny's father stood up.

Penny raced out of the house; she ran down to the beach. She walked for miles along the beach and came to the village where Sammy's school was. Children were coming out of the school. She watched as they ran over to their parents. A little boy was standing by himself. He looked so forlorn; Penny approached the school gates. It was Sammy.

Penny brought her hand up to her mouth, tears welled up. How could she be so cruel and leave him? She pushed open the gate and slowly walked up to him. She will never forget the smile he gave her.

"Sammy," Penny crouched down to him, he flung his arms around her waist and hugged her tightly. She kissed his head and whispered, "I am here Sammy".

After a few weeks, Penny became stronger, her parents went back home, so Penny had to go back to the shop. Penny noticed that no locals came in, except one, Moira Dalgleish. She was fierce, but Penny over the months had warmed to her.

Moira briskly walked into the shop, her trolley squeaking behind her. She was in her eighties and fit as a fiddle. Her white hair was tied into a bun.

Bear was asleep in his basket and raised his head when she passed him.

"Morning Penny," Moira went straight over to where the sweets were.

"Morning Moira," Penny sighed rubbing her forehead. Moira turned and looked at her.

"How are you doing?" Moira narrowed her eyes and slowly walked over to Penny.

"Good days and bad days…" Penny leant on the counter "Moira, can I ask you something?"

"Aye.." Moira pulled her trolley close to her.

"Why, are none of the locals coming into the shop?" Penny looked down at her.

Moira looked away.

"Moira…" Penny said slowly, tapping her fingers on the counter.

"Penny dear, you have to understand that the community here, are still in shock over Ethan and Ellen."

"I know, but why don't they come into the shop?" Penny sighed.

Moira came close to the counter and lightly tapped it with her finger.

"Penny, I am just going to say it. The feeling is, that since you came to the island bad things have happened and you have brought bad luck."

"So, they think I am a witch?" Penny huffed.

"No, it's just folk here are superstitious and narrow-minded."

"Maybe Sammy and I should move away..." Penny chewed on her thumbnail.

"Oh, don't be silly. Once the dust has settled, they will be back, just be patient...besides...you have more to worry about, than a few locals disliking you."

Moira pursed her lips together.

Penny leant back from Moira, taken aback by her bluntness.

"Worried about what?" Penny tilted her head.

Moira looked down at Penny's stomach.

"I would say eight weeks..." Moira gave a knowing look.

"Moira...how do you know?" Penny whispered, "Are you a witch?"

"No, not a witch, I was a midwife for forty years." Moira laughed and came around to Penny and pulled her to her.

"You have a bairn to think about now, the greatest joy any

woman can experience."

Penny burst into tears "How will I support Sammy and the baby. My only income is the shop and flat in London," Penny wiped her tears from her eyes.

"My Hamish was a fisherman, went out into that cruel sea and never came back. I supported five children. You will get through it, I did." Moira tapped Penny's shoulder.

The phone rang, and Penny clutched her chest with fright.

Moira gestured she answered it and walked to the back of the shop. Penny took a deep breath and answered the phone.

"Hello..." Penny said.

"You are going to have to speak up, I can't hear you," Penny raised her voice, she turned to Moira and pulled a face.

Penny gave up and ended the call.

"That is the fourth time today...." Penny spun the phone on the counter.

"Probably cold callers..." Moira gave a strained smile.

A few days later, Penny was in the shop, the weather was atrocious. Penny was looking at the books, Bear was constantly getting up and going over to the door and whining.

"I know, you will have a walk when the rain stops..." Penny groaned and went back to the books. Bear was now scratching at the door, Penny ignored him.

The door blew open with such force, that the bell flew to

the ground. Bear ran out, Penny chasing after him. A ferry had come in and passengers were making their way down the walkway onto the quayside.

Bear was barking and growling, Penny held onto his collar.

"Will you behave…" Penny shouted, the wind blowing her sideways. The boats moored in the port and were bobbing up and down.

He pulled so hard, that Penny couldn't hold on any longer and he broke free. He ran towards the ferry, Penny chasing him. There was one last passenger slowly making his way down the walkway. Bear bounded up to him.

Penny approached the person, apologising profusely, she pulled Bear away and made her way back to the shop. She walked in, the phone was ringing, she quickly walked over to the counter and answered it.

"I know, I couldn't talk the other day…" Penny walked around the counter, her back to the door.

"I know what you said, but I got you, Carlos. Can you tell me Ethan is safe?" Penny heard the floorboards behind her creak, she slowly turned, Uncle James was standing at the counter.

Penny dropped the phone.

"Care to tell me what the hell is going on?" he roared.

The End

VICTORIA LAWRENCE-SMITH

The concluding book will available 2023

Printed in Great Britain
by Amazon